PENGUIN BOOKS

IN THE SKIN OF A LION

Michael Ondaatje was born in Ceylon (now Sri Lanka) in 1943. His novels include *Coming through Slaughter*, about the jazz musician Buddy Bolden, *The Collected Works of Billy the Kid,* and *Running in the Family*, a family memoir. Among his books of poetry are *There's a Trick with a Knife I'm Learning to Do, Secular Love,* and *The Cinnamon Peeler: Selected Poems.* His latest work is the novel, *The English Patient.* He lives in Toronto.

Books by Michael Ondaatje

POETRY

The Dainty Monsters

The Man with 7 Toes

The Collected Works of Billy the Kid

Rat Jelly

Elimination Dance

*There's a Trick with a Knife
I'm Learning to Do*

Secular Love

The Cinnamon Peeler: Selected Poems

PROSE

Coming through Slaughter

Running in the Family

The English Patient

In the Skin of a Lion

a novel

MICHAEL ONDAATJE

Penguin Books

PENGUIN BOOKS

Published by the Penguin Group

Penguin Books Canada Ltd, 10 Alcorn Avenue, Toronto, Ontario, Canada M4V 3B2

Penguin Books Ltd, 27 Wrights Lane, London W8 5TZ, England

Penguin Books USA Inc., 375 Hudson Street, New York, New York 10014, U.S.A.

Penguin Books Australia Ltd, Ringwood, Victoria, Australia

Penguin Books (NZ) Ltd, 182-190 Wairau Road, Auckland 10, New Zealand

Penguin Books Ltd, Registered Offices:
Harmondsworth, Middlesex, England

First published by McClelland and Stewart, 1987

Published in Penguin Books, 1988

Published in this edition by Penguin Books, 1994

1 3 5 7 9 10 8 6 4 2

Copyright © Michael Ondaatje, 1987
Photography for CWM by William Kent

All rights reserved

*Publisher's note: This book is a work of fiction. Names, characters, places and incidents either
are the product of the author's imagination or are used fictitiously, and any resemblance to actual
persons living or dead, events, or locales is entirely coincidental.*

Manufactured in Canada

Canadian Cataloguing in Publication Data
Ondaatje, Michael, 1943 -
In the skin of a lion

ISBN 0-14-024039-X
I. Title
PS8529.N283I6   C813'.54   C88-094131-6
PR9199.3.053I6

Except in the United States of America, this book is sold subject to the condition that it
shall not, by way of trade or otherwise, be lent, re-sold, hired out, or otherwise circulated
without the publisher's prior consent in any form of binding or cover other than that in
which it is published and without a similar condition including this condition being
imposed on the subsequent purchaser.

Grateful acknowledgment is made for permission to reprint previously published song lyrics
from "Up Jumped You with Love © C.R. Publishing Company and "I Can't Get Started"
© Chappell Music Company. The lines from *The Epic of Gilgamesh* are from the N.K.
Sandars translation (Penguin, 1960). Two sentences on the photographs of Lewis Hine are
by Judith Mara Gutman from her essay "Lewis Hine and the American Social Conscience"
(1969). Two sentences have been used from the journals of Anne Wilkinson. Lines from
Martha Ostenso's *Wild Geese* are from the 1925 McClelland and Stewart edition.

This book is in memory of Michel Lambeth,
Sharon Stevenson, and Bill and Michal Acres

And for Linda, and Sarah and David

I'd like to express my gratitude to The John Simon Guggenheim Foundation who gave me a grant during the writing of this book. Also to the Ontario Arts Council, the El Basha Restaurant, the Multicultural History Society of Ontario, and Glendon College, York University.

I would also like to thank Margo Teasdale, George and Ruth Grant, Donya Peroff, Rick Haldenby, Paul Thompson, and Lillian Petroff. Also Ian Radforth for his work on Finnish lumber camp workers. A special thank you to Ellen Seligman.

*　　　*　　　*

The joyful will stoop with sorrow, and when
you have gone to the earth I will let my hair
grow long for your sake, I will wander through
the wilderness in the skin of a lion.

THE EPIC OF GILGAMESH

Never again will a single story be told
as though it were the only one.

JOHN BERGER

This is a story a young girl gathers in a car during the early hours of the morning. She listens and asks questions as the vehicle travels through darkness. Outside, the countryside is unbetrayed. The man who is driving could say, "In that field is a castle," and it would be possible for her to believe him.

She listens to the man as he picks up and brings together various corners of the story, attempting to carry it all in his arms. And he is tired, sometimes as elliptical as his concentration on the road, at times overexcited – "Do you see?" He turns to her in the faint light of the speedometer.

Driving the four hours to Marmora under six stars and a moon.

She stays awake to keep him company.

1

LITTLE SEEDS

IF HE IS AWAKE early enough the boy sees the men walk past the farmhouse down First Lake Road. Then he stands at the bedroom window and watches: he can see two or three lanterns between the soft maple and the walnut tree. He hears their boots on gravel. Thirty loggers, wrapped up dark, carrying axes and small packages of food which hang from their belts. The boy walks downstairs and moves to a window in the kitchen where he can look down the driveway. They move from right to left. Already they seem exhausted, before the energy of the sun.

Sometimes, he knows, this collection of strangers will meet the cows being brought in from a pasture barn for milking and there will be a hushed politeness as they stand to the side of the road holding up the lanterns (one step back and they will be in a knee-high snowdrift), to let the cows lazily pass them on the narrow road. Sometimes the men put their hands on the warm flanks of these animals and receive their heat as they pass. They put their thin-gloved hands on these black and white creatures, who are barely discernible in the last of the night's darkness. They must do this gently, without any sense of attack or right. They do not own this land as the owner of the cows does.

The holsteins pass the silent gauntlet of men. The farmer who follows the cows nods. He passes this strange community most mornings during the winter months, the companionship a silent comfort to him in the dark of five A.M. – for he has been rounding up cattle for over an hour to take them to the milking barns.

The boy who witnesses this procession, and who even dreams about it, has also watched the men working a mile away in the grey trees. He has heard their barks, heard their axes banging into the cold wood as if into metal, has seen a fire beside the creek where water is molecular and grey under the thin ice.

The sweat moves between their hard bodies and the cold clothes. Some die of pneumonia or from the sulphur in their lungs from the mills they work in during other seasons. They sleep in the shacks behind the Bellrock Hotel and have little connection with the town.

Neither the boy nor his father has ever been into those dark rooms, into a warmth which is the odour of men. A raw table, four bunks, a window the size of a torso. These are built each December and dismantled the following spring. No one in the town of Bellrock really knows where the men have come from. It takes someone else, much later, to tell the boy that. The only connection the loggers have with the town is when they emerge to skate along the line of river, on homemade skates, the blades made of old knives.

For the boy the end of winter means a blue river, means the disappearance of these men.

*   *   *

He longs for the summer nights, for the moment when he turns out the lights, turns out even the small cream funnel in the hall near the room where his father sleeps. Then the house is in

8

darkness except for the bright light in the kitchen. He sits down at the long table and looks into his school geography book with the maps of the world, the white sweep of currents, testing the names to himself, mouthing out the exotic. *Caspian. Nepal. Durango.* He closes the book and brushes it with his palms, feeling the texture of the pebbled cover and its coloured dyes which create a map of Canada.

Later, he walks through the dark living room, his hand stretched out in front of him, and returns the book to a shelf. He stands in darkness, rubbing his arms to bring energy back into his body. He is forcing himself to stay awake, take his time. It is still hot and he is naked to the waist. He walks back into the bright kitchen and moves from window to window to search out the moths pinioned against the screens, clinging to brightness. From across the fields they will have seen this one lighted room and travelled towards it. A summer night's inquiry.

Bugs, plant hoppers, grasshoppers, rust-dark moths. Patrick gazes on these things which have navigated the warm air above the surface of the earth and attached themselves to the mesh with a muted thunk. He'd heard them as he read, his senses tuned to such noises. Years later at the Riverdale Library he will learn how the shining leaf-chafers destroy shrubbery, how the flower beetles feed on the juice of decaying wood or young corn. There will suddenly be order and shape to these nights. Having given them fictional names he will learn their formal titles as if perusing the guest list for a ball – the Spur-throated Grasshopper! The Archbishop of Canterbury!

Even the real names are beautiful. Amber-winged skimmer. Bush cricket. Throughout the summer he records their visits and sketches the repeaters. Is it the same creature? He crayons the orange wings of the geometer into his notebook, the lunar

9

moth, the soft brown – as if rabbit fur – of the tussock moth. He will not open the screen and capture their pollened bodies. He did this once and the terrified thrash of the moth – a brown-pink creature who released coloured dust on his fingers – scared them both.

Up close they are prehistoric. The insect jaws munch. Are they eating something minute or is it subliminal – the way his father chews his tongue when in the fields. The kitchen light radiates through their porous wings; even those that are squat, like the peach-green aphid, appear to be constructed of powder.

Patrick pulls a double-ocarina from his pocket. Outside he will not waken his father, the noise will simply drift up into the arms of soft maple. Perhaps he can haunt these creatures. Perhaps they are not mute at all, it is just a lack of range in his hearing. (When he was nine his father discovered him lying on the ground, his ear against the hard shell of cow shit inside which he could hear several bugs flapping and knocking.) He knows the robust calls from the small bodies of cicadas, but he wants conversation – the language of damsel flies who need something to translate their breath the way he uses the ocarina to give himself a voice, something to leap with over the wall of this place.

Do they return nightly to show him something? Or does he haunt them? In the way he steps from the dark house and at the doorway of the glowing kitchen says to the empty fields, *I am here. Come and visit me.*

He was born into a region which did not appear on a map until 1910, though his family had worked there for twenty years and the land had been homesteaded since 1816.

In the school atlas the place is pale green and nameless. The river slips out of an unnamed lake and is a simple blue line until it becomes the Napanee twenty-five miles to the south, and, only because of logging, will eventually be called Depot Creek. "Deep Eau."

His father works for two or three farms, cutting wood, haying, herding cattle. The cows cross the river twice a day – in the morning they wander to the land south of the creek and in the afternoon they are rounded up for milking. In winter the animals are taken down the road to a pasture barn, though once a cow headed towards the river longing for back pasture.

They do not miss it for two hours and then his father guesses where it has gone. He runs towards the river yelling to the boy Patrick to follow with the field horses. Patrick is bareback on a horse leading the other by the rope, urging them on through the deep snow. He sees his father through the bare trees as he rides down the slope towards the swimming hole.

In mid-river, half-submerged in the ice, is the neighbouring farmer's holstein. There is no colour. The dry stalks of dead mulleins, grey trees, and the swamp now clean and white. His father with a rope around his shoulders creeps on his hands and knees across the ice towards the black and white shape. The cow heaves, splitting more ice, and cold water seeps up. Hazen Lewis pauses, calming the animal, then creeps on. He must get the rope under the body twice. Patrick moves forward slowly till he kneels on the other side of the cow. His father puts his left hand on the neck of the animal and plunges his right arm into the freezing water as low as he can go beneath the body. On the other side Patrick puts an arm in and waves it back and forth trying to come in contact with the rope. They cannot reach each other. Patrick lies on the ice so his arm and shoulder can go deeper, his wrist already starting to numb, and he thinks

11

that soon he will not be able to feel the rope even if it brushes against him.

The cow shifts and water soaks into the boy's coat, through to his chest. His father pulls back and the two of them kneel on either side of the cow and swing their wet arms, beating them against their chests. They don't speak. They must work as quickly as possible. His father puts his ungloved hand against the cow's ear to collect the animal's heat. He lies down sideways on the ice and plunges his arm down again, the water inches from his face. Patrick, in a mirror image, swirls his hand underwater but again there is nothing to touch. "I'm going under now. You've got to get it fast," his father says, and Patrick sees his father's trunk twitch and his head go into the icy water. Patrick's hand clutches his father's other arm on top of the cow, holding it tightly.

Then Patrick puts his head into the water and reaches out. He touches his father's wrist under the cow. He dares not let go and moves his hand carefully until he grips the thick braided rope. He pulls at it but it won't move. He realizes his father in going down deeper has somehow got his body over the rope, that he's lying on it. Patrick will not let go, though he is running out of air. His father gasps out of the water, lies on his back on the ice, and breathes hard past the ache in his eyes, then is suddenly aware of what he is lying on and rolls away, freeing the rope. Patrick pulls, using his foot now to jerk himself up out of the water, and he slithers over the ice away from the cow.

He sits up and sees his father and puts his arms up in a victory gesture. His father is frantically trying to get water out of his ears and off his eyes before it freezes in the air and Patrick uses his dry sleeve and does the same, shrinking his hand back into the jacket, prodding the cloth into his ears. He can feel the ice on his chin and neck already forming but he doesn't worry

12

about that. His father scuttles back to shore and returns with a second rope. This one he attaches to the first rope, and Patrick hauls it towards himself under the cow, so both ropes are now circled around the animal.

Patrick looks up – at the grey rock of the swimming hole, the oak towering over the dirty brush that spikes out of the snow. There is a clear blue sky. The boy feels as if he has not seen these things in years. Till this moment there was just his father, the black and white shape of the cow, and that terrible black water which cut into his eyes when he opened them down there.

His father attaches the ropes to the horses. The face of the half-submerged cow, a giant eye lolling, seems unconcerned. Patrick expects it to start chewing in complete boredom. He lifts its lip and puts his cold fingers against the gums to steal heat. Then he crawls to the bank.

Holding each of the horses by the halter he and his father yell encouragement to them. The horses do not even hesitate at the weight they are pulling. From the bank he sees the cow's tongue slide out, its complacent look for the first time replaced by concern as it is dragged towards the shoreline, breaking ice as it cuts a path. About ten feet from the bank where the ice is thicker the body tightens against the ropes. The horses stop. He and his father switch them, and they break into a trot. Then the whole cow magically emerges out of the ice and is dragged on its side, its four legs straight and hard in the air, dragged uncompromisingly onto the shore over the brown mulleins.

They let the horses go. He and his father try to untie the ropes on the cow but it is too difficult and his father brings out a knife and cuts the ropes away. The animal lies there snorting its steam into the cold air, then stumbles up and stands watching them. More than anything Patrick is surprised at his father who

13

is obsessed with not wasting things. He has lectured the boy several times on saving rope. Always unknot. Never cut! Bringing out his knife and slicing the rope to pieces is an outrageous, luxurious act.

They begin to run back home, looking behind them to see if the cow is following. The boy gasps, "If she goes into the ice again I'm not doing a thing." "Neither am I," yells his father, laughing. By the time they reach their back kitchen, it is almost dark and they have pains in their stomachs.

In the house Hazen Lewis lights the naphtha lamp and builds a fire. The boy shivers during dinner and the father tells the boy he can sleep with him. In bed later on, they do not acknowledge each other apart from sharing the warmth under the blanket. His father lies so still Patrick doesn't know if he is asleep or awake. The boy looks towards the kitchen and its dying fire.

He imagines himself through the winter until he is a white midsummer shadow beside his father. In summer his father drips gasoline onto the caterpillar tents and sets them on fire. *Flof.* The grey cobweb skins collapse into flame. Caterpillars drop onto grass, the acrid burn smell is in the roof of the boy's mouth. Two of them meticulously search a field in the evening light. Patrick points to a nest his father has missed and they walk deeper into the pasture.

He is almost asleep. In the darkness another flame ignites then withers into nothing.

*   *   *

In the drive-shed Hazen Lewis outlined the boy's body onto the plank walls with green chalk. Then he tacked wires back and forth across the outline as if realigning the veins in his son's frame. Muscles of cordite and the spine a tributary of the black powder fuse. This is how the boy remembers his father, studying the outline which the boy has just stepped away from as the lit fuse smoulders up and blows out a section of plank where the head had been.

Hazen Lewis was an abashed man, withdrawn from the world around him, uninterested in the habits of civilization outside his own focus. He would step up to his horse and assume it, as if it were a train, as if flesh and blood did not exist.

In winter months Patrick carried meals into the acreage north of the creek where his father, solitary, cut timber all day, minute in those white halls. And then when Patrick was fifteen, his father made the one leap of his life. At some moment, chopping into hemlock, hearing only the axe and its pivoting echo, he must have imagined the trees and permafrost and maple syrup ovens erupting up in one heave, the snow shaken off every branch in the woods around him. He stopped in midafternoon, walked home, unlaced his bear paws, and put away the axe forever. He wrote away for books, travelled into Kingston for materials. The explosion he saw in the woods had been an idea as he tugged his axe out of the hemlock. He bought dynamite and blasting caps and fuses, drew diagrams on the walls of the drive-shed, then carried the explosives into the woods. He laid the charges against rock and ice and trees. The detonator cap spat a flame into the cartridge and his eyes watched the snow collapse out of branches from the shudder in the air. Whatever was dislodged became a graph showing him the radius of the tremor.

Before the spring breakup Hazen Lewis rode down to the Rathbun Timber Company headquarters. He demonstrated his talent, moving a log into precisely the location he said it would go, exploding a half-ton of shale, and was hired along with the river drivers. He had secured a role for himself in the industry that took place along the Depot Lakes and the Napanee River. When the company closed down some years later he moved over and worked as a dynamiter in the feldspar mine excavations around Verona and Godfrey, hired by the Richardson Mines. In all his life the longest speech was the one made to the Rathbun staff when he told them what he could do and that as far as he was concerned there were only two sensible jobs in logging – being a dynamiter and being a cook.

Along the chain of Depot Lakes – from First Depot to Fifth Depot – the loggers arrived in winter and disappeared into shanty camps, walking twenty miles into land they did not know. All February and March at the centre of the lakes the pyramids of logs grew, hauled there by sleds. Before daybreak the men were working – through the worst storms, in weather far below zero – and they finished at six. The double-handed crosscut saw brought down the pines. The pulp cutters, bent double, had to saw the stumps just above the ground. This was the worst job. Some used the swede saw. It cut spruce at twice the speed of the crosscut, and when they moved to the next camp they rolled up the narrow blade, making new handles in whatever forest they arrived at.

In April, with the melting of the lake ice, the river drives began. This was the easiest and most dangerous work. From Bellrock to Napanee men were stationed wherever the river narrowed. Bridges or split rocks had two or three men always there in case of a jam. If a jammed log did not get fished out in time, the weight of others would pile up behind it and the whole length of the river would be padlocked. At this point the river

16

drivers could do nothing and a dispatcher was sent on horseback for the dynamiter. A twenty-foot log suddenly leaping out of the water and side-swiping a man, breaking his chest.

Hazen Lewis and his son rode up to the split rock. The large man walked around the logjam. He drilled in a plug of dynamite and lit the fuse. He got the boy to shout the warning and the logs went up into the air, onto the bank, and the river was free.

In difficult cases Patrick would remove his clothes and grease himself down with oil from the crankcase of the steam donkey. He dove into the ribbed water and swam among the logs. Every half-minute wherever he was he had to raise his hand to assure his father. Eventually the boy located the log his father had pointed to. He caught the charge thrown out to him, crimped the blasting cap onto the fuse with his teeth, and lit the powder.

He re-emerged from the water, walked back to the horses, and dried himself with the towels from the packsack, like his father not even turning around to watch. A river exploded behind him, the crows leafing up.

The drives lasted a month and he watched the men float by, riding the sawlogs with their large poles towards Yarker down to Napanee where the corralled logs were towed to the mills. He was always beside his father. Patrick lazed in a patch of sun by the bridge and they waited.

At noon the cook walked up First Lake Road with two dairy pails. One pail carried tea, the other contained thick pork sandwiches. The sound of the crows above the food was a signal, and men emerged from various bends in the river. When the meal was over the cook picked up two empty pails and stepped onto a log on the water's edge and floated back downstream to the camp. He stood up straight in mid-river, travelling at only the speed that the river wished. He would float under the bridge without altering his posture, though there was only an inch to spare, nodding to loggers on the bank, disheartened by the ever-present crows. He would step off at the camp at Goose Island with his shoes perfectly dry.

Hazen read his pamphlets. He dried the powdered cordite on a rock. He was sullen even in the company of his son. All his energy was with the fuse travelling at two minutes to the yard under floorboards, around the trunks of trees, and up into someone's pocket. He kept receiving that image in his mind. Could he do it? The fuse stitched into the cloth of the trouser leg. The man sleeping perhaps by a campfire, the fuse smouldering horizontal into his shirt pocket, blowing out the heart. In his preoccupations the fuse always zigzagged like a hound's nose along the ground, setting alight the ground cover till it was red lichen.

Hazen Lewis did not teach his son anything, no legend, no base of theory. The boy watched him prepare charges or pack equipment neatly back into his wooden case. His father wore no metal on him – not a watch or belt buckle. He was a man who with his few props had become self-sufficient, as invisible as possible. The explosions jostled logs out of the water unharmed. He left a track of half-inch holes in the granite all down the Depot Lakes system and along the Moira River system where he sometimes was hired. But these were as modest and minimal as they could be. A woodpecker's work. He never wore a hat. He was a big man, six-foot-six, a heavy body. He was a bad rider of horses and later on a bad driver of trucks. He could assemble river dynamite with his eyes closed. He was meticulous in washing his clothes every evening in case there were remnants, little seeds of explosive on his apparel. Patrick scorned this obsession. His father took off his shirt one evening and threw it onto the campfire. The shirt fizzed and sprayed sparks over the knees of the loggers. There were abrupt lessons like this.

It was strange for Patrick to realize later that he had learned important things, the way children learn from watching how adults angle a hat or approach a strange dog. He knew how much a piece of dynamite the size of a bullfrog could destroy. But he absorbed everything from a distance. The only moments his father was verbal was when calling square dances in the Yarker and Tamworth Hotels during the log drives. He was always called on and he walked up to the stage as if it were a duty and broke into verses, swirling around the guitars and fiddles, dropping in a last phrase tight before he hit the wall of the rhyme. Taciturn about everything else, his father was taciturn in his square-dance calling. His words would slide noncommittal over the dance floor, the boy watching at the edge and mouthing the phrases to himself. Not a muscle moved in the large body of his father as he stood there calling *"Little red wagon the axle draggin'."*

The unemotional tongue. Patrick could see himself on stage striding up and down, his arms bent and cocky. *"Birdie fly out and the crow fly in – crow fly out and give birdie a spin,"* he would mutter to himself, later, in the daylight.

One winter night when he was eleven years old, Patrick walked out from the long kitchen. A blue moth had pulsed on the screen, bathed briefly in light, and then disappeared into darkness. He did not think it would go far. He picked up the kerosene lamp and went out. A rare winter moth. It was scuffing along the snow as if injured and he could follow it easily. In the back garden he lost it, the turquoise moth arcing up into the sky beyond the radius of the kerosene light. What was a moth doing at this time of year? He hadn't seen any for months. It may have been bred in the chicken coop. He put the hurricane lamp onto a rock and looked over the fields. Among the trees in the distance he saw what looked like more bugs. Lightning bugs within the trees by the river. But this was winter! He moved forward with the lamp.

The distance was further than he thought. Snow above the ankles of his untied boots. One hand in a pocket, the other holding a lamp. And a moon lost in the thickness of clouds so it did not shine a path for him towards the trees. All that gave direction was a blink of amber. Already he knew it could not be lightning bugs. The last of the summer's fireflies had died somewhere in the folds of one of his handkerchiefs. (Years later, Clara making love to him in a car, catching his semen in a handkerchief and flinging it out onto bushes on the side of the road. *Hey, lightning bug!* he had said, laughing, offering no explanation.)

20

He waded through the snow, past outcrops of granite, and into the trees where the snow was not as deep. The lights still blinked in front of him. There was laughter. Now he knew what it was. He crept on into the familiar woods as if walking into, testing the rooms of a haunted house. He knew who it was but he did not know what he would see. Then he was at the river. He put the lamp down beside the oak and walked in darkness towards the bank.

The ice shone with light. It seemed for a moment that he had stumbled on a coven, or one of those strange druidic rituals – illustrations of which he had pored over in his favourite history book. But even to the boy of eleven, deep in the woods after midnight, this was obviously benign. Something joyous. A gift. There were about ten men skating, part of a game. One chased the others and as soon as someone was touched he became the chaser. Each man held in one hand a sheaf of cattails and the tops of these were on fire. This is what lit the ice and had blinked through the trees.

They raced, swerved, fell and rolled on the ice to avoid each other but never let go of the rushes. When they collided sparks fell onto the ice and onto their dark clothes. This is what caused the howls of laughter – one of them stationary, struggling to shake off a fragment that had fallen inside his sleeve, yelling out for the others to stop.

Patrick was transfixed. Skating the river at night, each of them moving like a wedge into the blackness magically revealing the grey bushes of the shore, *his* shore, *his* river. A tree branch reached out, its hand frozen in the ice, and one of them skated under it, crouching – cattails held behind him like a flaming rooster tail.

The boy knew they were the loggers from the camp. He longed to hold their hands and skate the length of the creek slowing down through cut rock and under bridges and into town with these men, knowing they would have to return to those dark cabins by the mill.

It was not just the pleasure of skating. They could have done that during the day. This was against the night. The hard ice was so certain, they could leap into the air and crash down and it would hold them. Their lanterns replaced with new rushes which let them go further past boundaries, speed! romance! one man waltzing with his fire. . . .

To the boy growing into his twelfth year, having lived all his life on that farm where day was work and night was rest, nothing would be the same. But on this night he did not trust either himself or these strangers of another language enough to be able to step forward and join them. He turned back through the trees and fields carrying his own lamp. Breaking the crust with each step seemed graceless and slow.

So at this stage in his life his mind raced ahead of his body.

THE BRIDGE

A TRUCK CARRIES fire at five A.M. through central Toronto, along Dundas Street and up Parliament Street, moving north. Aboard the flatbed three men stare into passing darkness – their muscles relaxed in this last half-hour before work – as if they don't own the legs or the arms jostling against their bodies and the backboard of the Ford.

Written in yellow over the green door is DOMINION BRIDGE COMPANY. But for now all that is visible is the fire on the flatbed burning over the three-foot by three-foot metal dish, cooking the tar in a cauldron, leaving this odour on the streets for anyone who would step out into the early morning and swallow the air.

The truck rolls burly under the arching trees, pauses at certain intersections where more workers jump onto the flatbed, and soon there are eight men, the fire crackling, hot tar now and then spitting onto the back of a neck or an ear. Soon there are twenty, crowded and silent.

The light begins to come out of the earth. They see their hands, the textures on a coat, the trees they had known were there. At the top of Parliament Street the truck turns east, passes the Rosedale fill, and moves towards the half-built viaduct.

The men jump off. The unfinished road is full of ruts and the fire and the lights of the truck bounce, the suspension wheezing. The truck travels so slowly the men are walking faster, in the cold dawn air, even though it is summer.

Later they will remove coats and sweaters, then by eleven their shirts, bending over the black rivers of tar in just their trousers, boots, and caps. But now the thin layer of frost is everywhere, coating the machines and cables, brittle on the rain puddles they step through. The fast evaporation of darkness. As light emerges they see their breath, the clarity of the air being breathed out of them. The truck finally stops at the edge of the viaduct, and its lights are turned off.

The bridge goes up in a dream. It will link the east end with the centre of the city. It will carry traffic, water, and electricity across the Don Valley. It will carry trains that have not even been invented yet.

Night and day. Fall light. Snow light. They are always working – horses and wagons and men arriving for work on the Danforth side at the far end of the valley.

There are over 4,000 photographs from various angles of the bridge in its time-lapse evolution. The piers sink into bedrock fifty feet below the surface through clay and shale and quicksand – 45,000 cubic yards of earth are excavated. The network of scaffolding stretches up.

Men in a maze of wooden planks climb deep into the shattered light of blond wood. A man is an extension of hammer, drill, flame. Drill smoke in his hair. A cap falls into the valley, gloves are buried in stone dust.

Then the new men arrive, the "electricals," laying grids of wire across the five arches, carrying the exotic three-bowl lights, and on October 18, 1918 it is completed. Lounging in mid-air.

The bridge. The bridge. Christened "Prince Edward." The Bloor Street Viaduct.

During the political ceremonies a figure escaped by bicycle through the police barriers. The first member of the public. Not the expected show car containing officials, but this one anonymous and cycling like hell to the east end of the city. In the photographs he is a blur of intent. He wants the virginity of it, the luxury of such space. He circles twice, the string of onions that he carries on his shoulder splaying out, and continues.

But he was not the first. The previous midnight the workers had arrived and brushed away officials who guarded the bridge in preparation for the ceremonies the next day, moved with their own flickering lights – their candles for the bridge dead – like a wave of civilization, a net of summer insects over the valley.

And the cyclist too on his flight claimed the bridge in that blurred movement, alone and illegal. Thunderous applause greeted him at the far end.

On the west side of the bridge is Bloor Street, on the east side is Danforth Avenue. Originally cart roads, mud roads, planked in 1910, they are now being tarred. Bricks are banged into the earth and narrow creeks of sand are poured in between them. The tar is spread. *Bitumiers, bitumatori,* tarrers, get onto their knees and lean their weight over the wooden block irons, which arc and sweep. The smell of tar seeps through the porous body of their clothes. The black of it is permanent under the nails.

They can feel the bricks under their kneecaps as they crawl backwards towards the bridge, their bodies almost horizontal over the viscous black river, their heads drunk within the fumes.

Hey, Caravaggio!

The young man gets up off his knees and looks back into the sun. He walks to the foreman, lets go of the two wooden blocks he is holding so they hang by the leather thongs from his belt, bouncing against his knees as he walks. Each man carries the necessities of his trade with him. When Caravaggio quits a year later he will cut the thongs with a fish knife and fling the blocks into the half-dry tar. Now he walks back in a temper and gets down on his knees again. Another fight with the foreman.

All day they lean over tar, over the twenty yards of black river that has been spread since morning. It glistens and eases in sunlight. Schoolkids grab bits of tar and chew them, first cooling the pieces in their hands, then popping them into their mouths. It concentrates the saliva for spitting contests. The men plunk cans of beans into the blackness to heat them up for their lunch.

In winter, snow removes the scent of tar, the scent of pitched cut wood. The Don River floods below the unfinished bridge, ice banging at the feet of the recently built piers. On winter mornings men fan out nervous over the whiteness. Where does the earth end? There are flares along the edge of the bridge on winter nights – worst shift of all – where they hammer the nails in through snow. The bridge builders balance on a strut, the flares wavering behind them, aiming their hammers towards the noise of a nail they cannot see.

*   *   *

The last thing Rowland Harris, Commissioner of Public Works, would do in the evenings during its construction was have himself driven to the edge of the viaduct, to sit for a while. At midnight the half-built bridge over the valley seemed deserted – just lanterns tracing its outlines. But there was always a night shift of thirty or forty men. After a while Harris removed himself from the car, lit a cigar, and walked onto the bridge. He loved this viaduct. It was his first child as head of Public Works, much of it planned before he took over but he had bullied it through. It was Harris who envisioned that it could carry not just cars but trains on a lower trestle. It could also transport water from the east-end plants to the centre of the city. Water was Harris' great passion. He wanted giant water mains travelling across the valley as part of the viaduct.

He slipped past the barrier and walked towards the working men. Few of them spoke English but they knew who he was. Sometimes he was accompanied by Pomphrey, an architect, the strange one from England who was later to design for Commissioner Harris one of the city's grandest buildings – the water filtration plant in the east end.

For Harris the night allowed scope. Night removed the limitations of detail and concentrated on form. Harris would bring Pomphrey with him, past the barrier, onto the first stage of the bridge that ended sixty yards out in the air. The wind moved like something ancient against them. All men on the bridge had to buckle on halter ropes. Harris spoke of his plans to this five-foot-tall Englishman, struggling his way into Pomphrey's brain. Before the real city could be seen it had to be imagined, the way rumours and tall tales were a kind of charting.

One night they had driven there at eleven o'clock, crossed the barrier, and attached themselves once again to the rope harnesses. This allowed them to stand near the edge to study the progress of the piers and the steel arches. There was a fire on the bridge where the night workers congregated, flinging logs and other remnants onto it every so often, warming themselves before they walked back and climbed over the edge of the bridge into the night.

They were working on a wood-facing for the next pier so that concrete could be poured in. As they sawed and hammered, wind shook the light from the flares attached to the side of the abutment. Above them, on the deck of the bridge, builders were carrying huge Ingersoll-Rand air compressors and cables.

An April night in 1917. Harris and Pomphrey were on the bridge, in the dark wind. Pomphrey had turned west and was suddenly stilled. His hand reached out to touch Harris on the shoulder, a gesture he had never made before.

    – Look!

Walking on the bridge were five nuns.

Past the Dominion Steel castings wind attacked the body directly. The nuns were walking past the first group of workers at the fire. The bus, Harris thought, must have dropped them off near Castle Frank and the nuns had, with some confusion at that hour, walked the wrong way in the darkness.

They had passed the black car under the trees and talking cheerfully stepped past the barrier into a landscape they did not know existed – onto a tentative carpet over the piers, among the night labourers. They saw the fire and the men. A few tried to wave them back. There was a mule attached to a wagon. The hiss and jump of machines made the ground under them lurch. A smell of creosote. One man was washing his face in a barrel of water.

The nuns were moving towards a thirty-yard point on the bridge when the wind began to scatter them. They were thrown against the cement mixers and steam shovels, careering from side to side, in danger of going over the edge.

Some of the men grabbed and enclosed them, pulling leather straps over their shoulders, but two were still loose. Harris and Pomphrey at the far end looked on helplessly as one nun was lifted up and flung against the compressors. She stood up shakily and then the wind jerked her sideways, scraping her along the concrete and right off the edge of the bridge. She disappeared into the night by the third abutment, into the long depth of air which held nothing, only sometimes a rivet or a dropped hammer during the day.

Then there was no longer any fear on the bridge. The worst, the incredible, had happened. A nun had fallen off the Prince Edward Viaduct before it was even finished. The men covered in wood shavings or granite dust held the women against them. And Commissioner Harris at the far end stared along the mad pathway. This was his first child and it had already become a murderer.

The man in mid-air under the central arch saw the shape fall towards him, in that second knowing his rope would not hold them both. He reached to catch the figure while his other hand grabbed the metal pipe edge above him to lessen the sudden jerk on the rope. The new weight ripped the arm that held the pipe out of its socket and he screamed, so whoever might have heard him up there would have thought the scream was from the falling figure. The halter thulked, jerking his chest up to his throat.

The right arm was all agony now – but his hand's timing had been immaculate, the grace of the habit, and he found himself a moment later holding the figure against him dearly.

He saw it was a black-garbed bird, a girl's white face. He saw this in the light that sprayed down inconstantly from a flare fifteen yards above them. They hung in the halter, pivoting over the valley, his broken arm loose on one side of him, holding the woman with the other. Her body was in shock, her huge eyes staring into the face of Nicholas Temelcoff.

Scream, please, Lady, he whispered, the pain terrible. He asked her to hold him by the shoulders, to take the weight off his one good arm. A sway in the wind. She could not speak though her eyes glared at him bright, just staring at him. *Scream, please.* But she could not.

During the night, the long chutes through which wet concrete slid were unused and hung loose so the open spouts wavered a few feet from the valley floor. The tops of these were about ten feet from him now. He knew this without seeing them, even though they fell outside the scope of light. If they attempted to slide the chute their weight would make it vertical and dangerous. They would have to go further – to reach the lower-deck level of the bridge where there were structures built for possible water mains.

We have to swing. She had her hands around his shoulders now, the wind assaulting them. The two strangers were in each other's arms, beginning to swing wilder, once more, past the lip of the chute which had tempted them, till they were almost at the lower level of the rafters. He had his one good arm free. Saving her now would be her responsibility.

She was in shock, her face bright when they reached the lower level, like a woman with a fever. She was in no shape to be witnessed, her veil loose, her cropped hair open to the long wind down the valley. Once they reached the catwalk she saved him from falling back into space. He was exhausted. She held him and walked with him like a lover along the unlit lower parapet towards the west end of the bridge.

Above them the others stood around the one fire, talking agitatedly. The women were still tethered to the men and not looking towards the stone edge where she had gone over, falling in darkness. The one with that small scar against her nose . . . she was always falling into windows, against chairs. She was always unlucky.

The Commissioner's chauffeur slept in his car as Temelcoff and the nun walked past, back on real earth away from the bridge. Before they reached Parliament Street they cut south through the cemetery. He seemed about to faint and she held him against a gravestone. She forced him to hold his arm rigid, his fist clenched. She put her hands underneath it like a stirrup and jerked upwards so he screamed out again, her whole body pushing up with all of her strength, groaning as if about to lift him and then holding him, clutching him tight. She had seen the sweat jump out of his face. *Get me a shot. Get me. . . .* She removed her veil and wrapped the arm tight against his side. *Parliament and Dundas . . . few more blocks.* So she went down Parliament Street with him. Where she was going she didn't know. On Eastern Avenue she knocked at the door he pointed to. All these abrupt requests – scream, swing, knock, get me. Then a man opened the door and let them into the Ohrida Lake Restaurant. *Thank you, Kosta. Go back to bed, I'll lock it.* And the man, the friend, walked back upstairs.

She stood in the middle of the restaurant in darkness. The chairs and tables were pushed back to the edge of the room. Temelcoff brought out a bottle of brandy from under the counter and picked up two small glasses in the fingers of the same hand. He guided her to a small table, then walked back and, with a switch behind the zinc counter, turned on a light near her table. There were crests on the wall.

She still hadn't said a word. He remembered she had not even screamed when she fell. That had been him.

*   *   *

Nicholas Temelcoff is famous on the bridge, a daredevil. He is given all the difficult jobs and he takes them. He descends into the air with no fear. He is a solitary. He assembles ropes, brushes the tackle and pulley at his waist, and falls off the bridge like a diver over the edge of a boat. The rope roars alongside him, slowing with the pressure of his half-gloved hands. He is burly on the ground and then falls with terrific speed, grace, using the wind to push himself into corners of abutments so he can check driven rivets, sheering valves, the drying of the concrete under bearing plates and padstones. He stands in the air banging the crown pin into the upper cord and then shepherds the lower cord's slip-joint into position. Even in archive photographs it is difficult to find him. Again and again you see vista before you and the eye must search along the wall of sky to the speck of burned paper across the valley that is him, an exclamation mark, somewhere in the distance between bridge and river. He floats at the three hinges of the crescent-shaped steel arches. These knit the bridge together. The moment of cubism.

He is happiest at daily chores – ferrying tools from pier down to trestle, or lumber that he pushes in the air before him as if swimming in a river. He is a spinner. He links everyone. He meets them as they cling – braced by wind against the metal they are rivetting or the wood sheeting they hammer into – but he has none of their fear. Always he carries his own tackle, hunched under his ropes and dragging the shining pitons behind him. He sits on a coiled seat of rope while he eats his lunch on the bridge. If he finishes early he cycles down Parliament Street to the Ohrida Lake Restaurant and sits in the darkness of the room as if he has had enough of light. Enough of space.

His work is so exceptional and time-saving he earns one dollar an hour while the other bridge workers receive forty cents. There is no jealousy towards him. No one dreams of doing half the things he does. For night work he is paid $1.25, swinging up into the rafters of a trestle holding a flare, free-falling like a dead star. He does not really need to see things, he has charted all that space, knows the pier footings, the width of the crosswalks in terms of seconds of movement – 281 feet and 6 inches make up the central span of the bridge. Two flanking spans of 240 feet, two end spans of 158 feet. He slips into openings on the lower deck, tackles himself up to bridge level. He knows the precise height he is over the river, how long his ropes are, how many seconds he can free-fall to the pulley. It does not matter if it is day or night, he could be blindfolded. Black space is time. After swinging for three seconds he puts his feet up to link with the concrete edge of the next pier. He knows his position in the air as if he is mercury slipping across a map.

*　　　*　　　*

A South River parrot hung in its cage by the doorway of the Ohrida Lake Restaurant, too curious and interested in the events of the night to allow itself to be blanketed. It watched the woman who stood dead centre in the room in darkness. The man turned on one light behind the counter. Nicholas Temelcoff came over to the bird for a moment's visit after getting the drinks. "Well, Alicia, my heart, how are you?" And walked away not waiting for the bird's reply, the fingers of his left hand delicately holding the glasses, his arm cradling the bottle.

He muttered as if continuing his conversation with the bird, in the large empty room. From noon till two it was full of men, eating and drinking. Kosta the owner and his waiter performing raucous shows for the crowd – the boss yelling insults at the waiter, chasing him past customers. Nicholas remembered the first time he had come there. The dark coats of men, the arguments of Europe.

He poured a brandy and pushed it over to her. "You don't have to drink this but you can if you wish. Or see it as a courtesy." He drank quickly and poured himself another. "Thank you," he said, touching his arm curiously as if it were the arm of a stranger.

She shook her head to communicate it was not all right, that it needed attention.

"Yes, but not now. Now I want to sit here." There was a silence between them. "Just to drink and talk quietly. . . . It is always night here. People step in out of sunlight and must move slow in the darkness."

He drank again. "Just for the pain." She smiled. "Now music." He stood up free of the table as he spoke and went behind the counter and turned the wireless on low. He spun the dial till there was bandstand. He sat down again opposite her. "Lot of pain. But I feel good." He leaned back in his chair, holding up his glass. "Alive." She picked up her glass and drank.

"Where did you get that scar?" He pointed his thumb to the side of her nose. She pulled back.

"Don't be shy . . . talk. You must talk." He wanted her to come out to him, even in anger, though he didn't want anger. Feeling such ease in the Ohrida Lake Restaurant, feeling the struts of the chair along his back, her veil tight on his arm. He just wanted her there near him, night all around them, where he could look after her, bring her out of the shock with some grace.

"I got about twenty scars," he said, "all over me. One on my ear here." He turned and leaned forward so the wall-light fell onto the side of his head. "See? Also this under my chin, that also broke my jaw. A coiling wire did that. Nearly kill me, broke my jaw. Lots more. My knees. . . ." He talked on. Hot tar burns on his arm. Nails in his calves. Drinking up, pouring her another shot, the woman's song on the radio. She heard the lyrics underneath Temelcoff's monologue as he talked and half mouthed the song and searched into her bright face. Like a woman with a fever.

This is the first time she has sat in a Macedonian bar, in any bar, with a drinking man. There is a faint glow from the varnished tables, the red checkered tablecloths of the day are folded and stacked. The alcove with its serving counter has an awning hanging over it. She realizes the darkness represents a Macedonian night where customers sit outside at their tables. Light can come only from the bar, the stars, the clock dressed in its orange and red electricity. So when customers step in at any time, what they are entering is an old courtyard of the Balkans. A violin. Olive trees. Permanent evening. Now the arbour-like wallpaper makes sense to her. Now the parrot has a language.

He talked on, slipping into phrases from the radio songs which is how he learned his words and pronunciations. He talked about himself, tired, unaware his voice split now into two languages, the woman hearing everything he said and trying to remember it all. He could see her eyes were alive, interpreting the room. He noticed the almost-tap of her finger to the radio music.

The blue eyes stayed on him as he moved, leaning his head against the wall. He drank, his breath deep into the glass so the fumes would hit his eyes and the sting of it keep him awake. Then he looked back at her. How old was she? Her brown hair so short, so new to the air. He wanted to coast his hand through it.

"I love your hair," he said. "Thank you . . . for the help. For taking the drink."

She leaned forward earnestly and looked at him, searching out his face now. Words just on the far side of her skin, about to fall out. Wanting to know his name which he had forgotten to tell her. "I love your hair." His shoulder was against the wall and he was trying to look up. Then his eyes were closed. So deeply asleep he would be gone for hours. She could twist him around like a puppet and he wouldn't waken.

She felt as if she were the only one alive in this building. In such formal darkness. There was a terrible taste from that one drink still on her tongue, so she walked behind the zinc counter, turning on the tap to wash out her mouth. She moved the dial of the radio around a bit but brought it back securely to the same station. She was looking for that song he had half sung along with earlier, the voice of the singer strangely powerful and lethargic. She saw herself in the mirror. A woman whose hair was showing, caught illicit. She did what he had wanted to do. She ran her hand over her hair briefly. Then turned from her image.

Leaning forward, she laid her face on the cold zinc, the chill there even past midnight. Upon her cheek, her eyelid. She let her skull roll to cool her forehead. The zinc was an edge of another country. She put her ear against the grey ocean of it. Its memory of a day's glasses. The spill and the wiping cloth. Confessional. Tabula Rasa.

At the table she positioned the man comfortably so he would not fall on his arm. *What is your name?* she whispered. She bent down and kissed him, then began walking around the room. This orchard. Strangers kiss softly as moths, she thought.

*　　*　　*

In certain weather, when fog fills the valley, the men stay close to each other. They arrive for work and walk onto a path that disappears into whiteness. What country exists on the other side? They move in groups of three or four. Many have already died during the building of the bridge. But especially on mornings like this there is a prehistoric fear, a giant bird lifting one of the men into the air. . . .

Nicholas has removed his hat, stepped into his harness, and dropped himself off the edge, falling thirty feet down through fog. He hangs under the spine of the bridge. He can see nothing, just his hands and the yard of pulley-rope above him. Six in the morning and he's already lost to that community of men on the bridge who are also part of the fairy tale.

He is parallel to the lattice-work of hanging structures. Now he enters the cages of steel and wood like a diver entering a sunken vessel that could at any moment tip over into deeper fracture zones of the sea floor. Nicholas Temelcoff works as the guy derricks raise and lower the steel – assembling it further out towards the next pier. He directs the steel through the fog. He is a fragment at the end of the steel bone the derrick carries on the end of its sixty-foot boom. The steel and Nicholas are raised up to a temporary track and from there the 'travellers' handle it. On the west end of the viaduct a traveller is used to erect the entire 150-foot span. The travellers are twin derricks fitted with lattice-work booms that can lift twelve tons into any position, like a carrot off the nose of the most recently built section of the bridge.

Nicholas is not attached to the travellers, his rope and pulleys link up only with the permanent steel of a completed section of the bridge. Travellers have collapsed twice before this and fallen to the floor of the valley. He is not attaching himself to a falling structure. But he hangs beside it, in the blind whiteness, slipping down further within it until he can shepherd the new ribs of steel onto the end of the bridge. He bolts them in, having to free-fall in order to use all of his weight for the final turns of the giant wrench. He allows ten feet of loose rope on the pulley, attaches the wrench, then drops onto the two-foot handle, going down with it, and jars with the stiffening of the bolt, falling off into the air, and jars again when he reaches the end of the rope. He pulleys himself up and does it again. After ten minutes every bone feels broken – the air he stops in feels hard as concrete, his spine aching where the harness pulls him short.

He rises with the traveller from the lower level, calling out numbers to the driver above him through the fog, alongside the clattering of the woodwork he holds onto, the creaks and bends of the lattice drowning out his call of *one – two – three – four* which is the only language he uses. He was doing this once when a traveller collapsed at night – the whole structure – the rope shredding around him. He let go, swinging into the darkness, *anywhere* that might be free of the fifteen tons of falling timber which crashed onto the lower level and then tumbled down into the valley, rattling and banging in space like a trolley full of metal. And on the far end of the swing, he knew he had escaped the timber, but not necessarily the arm-thick wires that were now uncoiling free, snaking powerfully in every direction through the air. On his return swing he curled into a ball to avoid them, hearing the wires whip laterally as they completed the energy of the break. His predecessor had been killed in a similar accident, cut, the upper half of his body found an hour later, still hanging in the halter.

By eight A.M. the fog is burned up and the men have already been working for over two hours. A smell of tar descends to Nicholas as workers somewhere pour and begin to iron it level. He hangs waiting for the whistle that announces the next journey of the traveller. Below him is the Don River, the Grand Trunk, the CN and CP railway tracks, and Rosedale Valley Road. He can see the houses and work shacks, the beautiful wooden sheeting of the abutment which looks like a revival tent. Wind dries the sweat on him. He talks in English to himself.

*   *   *

She takes the first step out of the Ohrida Lake Restaurant into the blue corridor – the narrow blue lane of light that leads to the street. What she will become she becomes in that minute before she is outside, before she steps into the six-A.M. morning. The parrot Alicia regards her departure and then turns its attention back to the man asleep in the chair, one arm on the table, palm facing up as if awaiting donations, his head against the wall beside a crest. He is in darkness now, the open palm callused and hard. Five years earlier or ten years into the future the woman would have smelled the flour in his hair, his body having slept next to the dough, curling around it so his heat would make it rise. But now it was the hardness of his hands, the sound of them she would remember like wood against glass.

*   *   *

Commissioner Harris never speaks to Nicholas Temelcoff but watches often as he hooks up and walks at the viaduct edge listening to the engineer Taylor's various instructions. He appears abstracted but Harris knows he listens carefully. Nicholas never catches anyone's eye, as if he must hear the orders nakedly without seeing a face around the words.

His eyes hook to objects. Wood, a railing, a rope clip. He eats his sandwiches without looking at them, watching instead a man attaching a pulley to the elevated railings or studying the expensive leather on the shoes of the architects. He drinks water from a corked green bottle and his eyes are focused a hundred feet away. He never realizes how often he is watched by others. He has no clue that his gestures are extreme. He has no portrait of himself. So he appears to Harris and the others as a boy: say, a fanatic about toy cars, some stage they all passed through years ago.

Nicholas strides the parapet looking sideways at the loops of rope and then, without pausing, steps into the clear air. Now there is for Harris nothing to see but the fizzing rope, a quick slither. Nicholas stops twenty feet down with a thud against his heart. Sometimes on the work deck they will hear him slowly begin to sing various songs, breaking down syllables and walking around them as if laying the clauses out like tackle on a pavement to be checked for worthiness, picking up one he fancies for a moment then replacing it with another. As with sight, because Nicholas does not listen to most conversations around him, he assumes no one hears him.

For Nicholas language is much more difficult than what he does in space. He loves his new language, the terrible barriers of it. "'Does she love me? – Absolutely! Do I love her? – Positively!'" Nicholas sings out to the forty-foot pipe he ferries across the air towards the traveller. *He* knows Harris. He *knows* Harris by the time it takes him to walk the sixty-four feet six inches from sidewalk to sidewalk on the bridge and by his expensive tweed coat that cost more than the combined weeks' salaries of five bridge workers.

The event that will light the way for immigration in North America is the talking picture. The silent film brings nothing but entertainment – a pie in the face, a fop being dragged by a bear out of a department store – all events governed by fate and timing, not language and argument. The tramp never changes the opinion of the policeman. The truncheon swings, the tramp scuttles through a corner window and disturbs the fat lady's ablutions. These comedies are nightmares. The audience emits horrified laughter as Chaplin, blindfolded, rollerskates near the edge of the unbalconied mezzanine. No one shouts to warn him. He cannot talk or listen. North America is still without language, gestures and work and bloodlines are the only currency.

But it was a spell of language that brought Nicholas here, arriving in Canada without a passport in 1914, a great journey made in silence. Hanging under the bridge, he describes the adventure to himself, just as he was told a fairy tale of Upper America by those who returned to the Macedonian villages, those first travellers who were the judas goats to the west.

Daniel Stoyanoff had tempted them all. In North America everything was rich and dangerous. You went in as a sojourner and came back wealthy – Daniel buying a farm with the compensation he had received for losing an arm during an accident in a meat factory. Laughing about it! Banging his other hand down hard onto the table and wheezing with laughter, calling them all fools, sheep! As if his arm had been a dry cow he had fooled the Canadians with.

Nicholas had been stunned by the simplicity of the contract. He could see Stoyanoff's body livid on the killing floor – standing in two inches of cow blood, screaming like nothing as much as cattle, his arm gone, his balance gone. He had returned to the village of Oschima, his sleeve flapping like a scarf, and with cash for the land. He had looked for a wife with two arms and settled down.

In ten years Daniel Stoyanoff had bored everyone in the village with his tall tales and he couldn't wait for children to grow up and become articulate so he could thrill them with his sojourner's story of Upper America. What Daniel told them was that he had in fact lost both arms in the accident, but he happened to be rooming with a tailor who was out of work and who had been, luckily, on the killing floors of Schnaufer's that morning. Dedora the tailor had pulled gut out of a passing cat, stitched Daniel's right arm back on, and then turned for the other but a scrap dog had run off with it, one of those dogs that lounged by the doorway. Whenever you looked up from cutting and slicing the carcasses you would see them, whenever you left work at the end of the day in your blood-soaked overalls and boots they followed you, licking and chewing your cuffs.

Stoyanoff's story was told to all children of the region at a certain age and he became a hero to them. *Look,* he would say, stripping off his shirt in the Oschima high street, irritating the customers of Petroff's outdoor bar once more, *look at what a good tailor Dedora was — no hint of stitches.* He drew an imaginary line around his good shoulder and the kids brought their eyes up close, then went over to his other shoulder and saw the alternative, the grotesque stump.

Nicholas was twenty-five years old when war in the Balkans began. After his village was burned he left with three friends on horseback. They rode one day and a whole night and another day down to Trikala, carrying food and a sack of clothes. Then they jumped on a train that was bound for Athens. Nicholas had a fever, he was delirious, needing air in the thick smoky compartments, wanting to climb up onto the roof. In Greece they bribed the captain of a boat a napoleon each to carry them over to Trieste. By now they all had fevers. They slept in the basement of a deserted factory, doing nothing, just trying to keep warm. There had to be no hint of illness before trying to get into Switzerland. They were six or seven days in the factory basement, unaware of time. One almost died from the high fevers. They slept embracing each other to keep warm. They talked about Daniel Stoyanoff's America.

On the train the Swiss doctor examined everyone's eyes and let the four friends continue over the border. They were in France. In Le Havre they spoke to the captain of an old boat that carried animals. It was travelling to New Brunswick.

Two of Nicholas' friends died on the trip. An Italian showed him how to drink blood in the animal pens to keep strong. It was a French boat called *La Siciliana.* He still remembered the name, remembered landing in Saint John and everyone thinking how primitive it looked. How primitive Canada was. They had to walk half a mile to the station where they were to be examined. They took whatever they needed from the sacks of the two who had died and walked towards Canada.

Their boat had been so filthy they were covered with lice. The steerage passengers put down their baggage by the outdoor taps near the toilets. They stripped naked and stood in front of their partners as if looking into a mirror. They began to remove the lice from each other and washed the dirt off with cold water and a cloth, working down the body. It was late November. They put on their clothes and went into the Customs sheds.

Nicholas had no passport, he could not speak a word of English. He had ten napoleons, which he showed them to explain he wouldn't be dependent. They let him through. He was in Upper America.

He took a train for Toronto, where there were many from his village; he would not be among strangers. But there was no work. So he took a train north to Copper Cliff, near Sudbury, and worked there in a Macedonian bakery. He was paid seven dollars a month with food and sleeping quarters. After six months he went to Sault Ste. Marie. He still could hardly speak English and decided to go to school, working nights in another Macedonian bakery. If he did not learn the language he would be lost.

The school was free. The children in the class were ten years old and he was twenty-six. He used to get up at two in the morning and make dough and bake till 8:30. At nine he would go to school. The teachers were all young ladies and were very good people. During this time in the Sault he had translation dreams – because of his fast and obsessive studying of English. In the dreams trees changed not just their names but their looks and character. Men started answering in falsettos. Dogs spoke out fast to him as they passed him on the street.

When he returned to Toronto all he needed was a voice for all this language. Most immigrants learned their English from recorded songs or, until the talkies came, through mimicking actors on stage. It was a common habit to select one actor and follow him throughout his career, annoyed when he was given a small part, and seeing each of his plays as often as possible – sometimes as often as ten times during a run. Usually by the end of an east-end production at the Fox or Parrot Theatres the actors' speeches would be followed by growing echoes as Macedonians, Finns, and Greeks repeated the phrases after a half-second pause, trying to get the pronunciation right.

This infuriated the actors, especially when a line such as "Who put the stove in the living room, Kristin?" – which had originally brought the house down – was now spoken simultaneously by at least seventy people and so tended to lose its spontaneity. When the matinee idol Wayne Burnett dropped dead during a performance, a Sicilian butcher took over, knowing his lines and his blocking meticulously, and money did not have to be refunded.

Certain actors were popular because they spoke slowly. Lethargic ballads, and a kind of blues where the first line of a verse is repeated three times, were in great demand. Sojourners walked out of their accent into regional American voices. Nicholas, unfortunately, would later choose Fats Waller as his model and so his emphasis on usually unnoticed syllables and the throwaway lines made him seem high-strung or dangerously anti-social or too loving.

But during the time he worked on the bridge, he was seen as a recluse. He would begin sentences in his new language, mutter, and walk away. He became a vault of secrets and memories.

Privacy was the only weight he carried. None of his cohorts really knew him. This man, awkward in groups, would walk off and leave strange clues about himself, like a dog's footprints on the snowed roof of a garage.

*   *   *

Hagh! A doctor attending his arm, this is what woke him, brought him out of his dream. *Hah!* It was six hours since he had fallen asleep. Kosta was there. He saw that the veil and his shirt had been cut open by the doctor. Somehow, they said, he had managed to get his arm back into the socket.

He jerked his hand to the veil, looking at it closely.

She had stayed until Kosta came down in the early morning. She talked to him about the arm, to get a doctor, she had to leave. She spoke? Yes yes. What did she sound like? Hah? What more did Kosta know about her? He mentioned her black skirt. Before he left, Nicholas looked around the bar and found strips of the black habit she had cut away to make a skirt for the street.

When he walks into the fresh air outside the Ohrida Lake Restaurant, on the morning after the accident on the bridge, he sees the landscape as something altered, no longer so familiar that it is invisible to him. Nicholas Temelcoff walks now seeing Parliament Street from the point of view of the woman – who had looked through his belt-satchel while he slept, found his wide wire shears, and used them to cut away the black lengths of her habit. When he walks out of the Ohrida Lake Restaurant that morning it is her weather he grows aware of. He knows he will find her.

There are long courtships which are performed in absence. This one is built perhaps on his remark about her hair or her almost-silent question as he was falling off some tower or bridge into sleep. The verge of sleep was always terrifying to Nicholas so he would drink himself into it blunting out the seconds of pure fear when he could not use his arms, would lie there knowing he'd witness the half-second fall before sleep, the fear of it greater than anything he felt on the viaduct or any task he carried out for the Dominion Bridge Company.

As he fell, he remembers later, he felt a woman's arm reaching for him, curious about his name.

He is aware of her now, the twin. What holds them together is not the act which saved her life but those moments since. The lost song on the radio. His offhand and relaxed flattery to a nun with regard to her beauty. Then he had leaned his head back, closed his eyes for too long, and slept.

A week later he rejoins the flatbed truck that carries the tar and fire, jumps on with the other men, and is back working at the bridge. His arm healed, he swings from Pier D to Pier C, ignores the stories he hears of the nun who disappeared. He lies supine on the end of his tether looking up towards the struts of the bridge, pivoting slowly. He knows the panorama of the valley better than any engineer. Like a bird. Better than Edmund Burke, the bridge's architect, or Harris, better than the surveyors of 1912 when they worked blind through the bush. The panorama revolves with him and he hangs in this long silent courtship, her absence making him look everywhere.

In a year he will open up a bakery with the money he has saved. He releases the catch on the pulley and slides free of the bridge.

THE SEARCHER

Patrick Lewis arrived in the city of Toronto as if it were land after years at sea. Growing up in the country had governed his childhood: the small village of Bellrock, the highway of river down which the log drivers came, drinking, working raucous, and in the spring leaving the inhabitants shocked within the silence. Now, at twenty-one, he had been drawn out from that small town like a piece of metal and dropped under the vast arches of Union Station to begin his life once more. He owned nothing, had scarcely any money. There was a piece of feldspar in his pocket that his fingers had stumbled over during the train journey. He was an immigrant to the city.

What remained in Patrick from his childhood were letters frozen inside mailboxes after ice storms. What he remembered was loving only things to do with colour, hating the whiteness, stepping into the warm brown universe of barns, the breath and steam of cattle rolling out, the acrid shit and urine he could summon up even now in the heart of Toronto. The smell had paraded grandly over his first seduction in a hay bed, the angry girl slapping him when both were full and guilty. What he remembered was frozen laundry, carrying overalls like a body into the kitchen and seating them in a chair, hoping his father would see them before they melted and lolled over the table.

Then summer. Blackflies and mosquitoes. Leaping not into hay but into the black underwater colour of creek, walking naked to the farmhouse, chewing rhubarb, clothes under one arm. You bit the glossy skin of the raw rhubarb and ripped its fibres open and sucked the flavour out. You put the smallest pellet of raspberry onto your tongue and opened it delicately with your teeth. You stood in a field on a hot day obsessed with this precise taste.

Now, in the city, he was new even to himself, the past locked away. He saw his image in the glass of telephone booths. He ran his hands over the smooth pink marble pillars that reached up into the rotunda. This train station was a palace, its niches and caverns an intimate city. He could be shaved, eat a meal, or have his shoes coloured.

He saw a man with three suitcases, well-dressed, shouting out in another language. The man's eyes burned through everyone who at first received his scream personally. But the phrases were for angels in the air to assist him or for demons to leave him. Two days later Patrick returned to pick up his luggage from a locker. He saw the man again, still unable to move from his safe zone, in a different suit, as if one step away was the quicksand of the new world.

Patrick sat on a bench and watched the tides of movement, felt the reverberations of trade. He spoke out his name and it struggled up in a hollow echo and was lost in the high air of Union Station. No one turned. They were in the belly of a whale.

When Ambrose Small, the millionaire, disappeared in 1919, it was discovered that the police had his Bertillon record. Between 1889 and 1923 the Bertillon identification system was used to locate criminals and missing persons. Bertillon's method consisted of the measurement of certain parts of the body: the length of head, width of head, length of right ear, length of left foot, length of left middle finger, the length of left forearm. In homes and prisons and mortuaries all over North America limbs were measured and the results sent in to the Toronto police. During the fever of the case over 5,000 people claimed to be Ambrose Small. They claimed they had amnesia, were kidnapped in a brown sack, were disfigured, were hidden in geological holes in the Scarborough Bluffs, were stretched to longer than five foot six inches on racks, were overfed, had all their hair removed, had their memories wiped clean by certain foods, had their pigmentation altered, were turned into women, had the length of their right ear changed, were in the meantime hungry and penniless and would someone mail $500 to Nelson, B.C., or Wichita, Kansas, or Cornerbrook, Newfoundland.

A woman in Hamilton saw Ambrose with his throat cut. She woke one morning to feel blood on the pillow, looked up and saw someone was sawing her neck, and she said I am Ambrose Small. Then she woke up again. Another had a vision that she was unlocking the safe at the Grand Opera House and saw a curled-up skeleton inside resting on documents.

The press leapt upon every possibility.

MYSTERY MAN OF NORTH RESEMBLES SMALL
– Star, May 27, 1921
Remains may be exhumed if further clues come to light.

SKELETON FOUND IN WHITBY FIELD
– Telegram, June 2, 1921
"The possibility that it might be Ambrose Small occurred to me when we were digging it up," Acting Chief Thomas reflected this evening.

IOWA DETECTIVE IS CERTAIN HE HAS FOUND A.J. SMALL
– Mail, August 16, 1921
John Brophy, Head of Brophy Detective Agency, Iowa, who was ousted from his job as Assistant Chief of Police, claims to have a man under guard whom he has identified as A.J. Small. Brophy said he would produce Small when the Canadian authorities are ready to pay the reward offered.

"The man is Small," he said.

The man was recovering from a pistol wound in the neck, concussion of the brain and minor injuries. Both his legs had been cut off near the knees.

"I will tell you what Small told me after he had identified his own picture," he said. " 'All I can remember is that there was a blow and then darkness, then terrible suffering. From then on I remembered nothing until I was brought here. I think I was in Omaha, that's all.' "

Between 1910 and 1919 Ambrose Small had been the jackal of Toronto's business world. He was a manipulator of deals and property, working his way up from nothing into the world of theatre management. He bought Toronto's Grand Opera House when he was twenty-eight years old, and then proceeded to buy theatres all over the province – in St. Catharines, Kingston, Arkona, Petrolia, Peterborough, and Paris, Ontario, until he held the whole web of theatre traffic in his outstretched arms. He built the Grand in London, Ontario – the largest theatre in North America, save for Shea's Hippodrome. He owned ninety-six theatres. He became a gambler at the track, obsessed with greyhounds.

He married Theresa Kormann, and in so doing alienated his sisters. His wife was a prohibitionist and Small offered her the theatre for one night a week and she put on temperance shows and nobody came. *"Pass by the open doorway, ignore the foul saloon,"* the chorus sang to a mostly empty auditorium. On other nights, performances of *Ben-Hur* and *Naughty Miss Louise* packed the theatre. In the Glen Road house, Small held appalling parties. Showgirls, live peacocks, staggered out drunk in the morning hours and strolled aimlessly home along the Rosedale streets – the chauffeurs of the rich following at a tactful distance in their car.

In Paris, Ontario, he met an actress named Clara Dickens and she became his lover. She was twenty-one years old and Small was thirty-five and he charmed her with his variousness. He was a spinner. He was bare-knuckle capitalism. He was a hawk who hovered over the whole province, swooping down for the kill, buying up every field of wealth, and eating the profit in mid-air. He was a jackal. This is what the press called him and he laughed at them, spun a thread around his critics and bought them up. Either he owned people or they were his enemies. No compatriots. No prisoners. In the tenth century, he liked to say, the price of a greyhound or a hawk was the same as that for a man.

Each morning he rose and walked to his offices at the Grand Theatre on Adelaide Street. He got there at least an hour before any of his staff and plotted out the day. This was the time he loved most, choreographing his schemes, theorizing on bids and counter-bids and interest rates and the breaking point of his adversaries. He pulled out an imported avocado pear, sliced it into thin green moons, and sat at his roll-top desk eating it and thinking. By the time his staff arrived he had worked out all possible scenarios at his empty desk. He went down to the barbershop, lay back, and was shaved and manicured. His day was over. The machine of Ambrose Small began to tick across the city.

With his lover Clara Dickens he was gregarious, generous, charming. Seeing him once or twice a week she knew the best of Ambrose. She steered him away from his peacock parties. They went on excursions. He bought hotels, he bought houses under different names all over Ontario. "I'm a thief," he'd say. "All thieves must plan their escape routes." The names of the towns, his pseudonyms, slipped memorized into his brain, unrecorded anywhere else. He bought or consumed, it seemed to Clara, anything he alighted on.

On December 16, 1919, Ambrose Small failed to keep an appointment. A million dollars had been taken from his bank account. He had either been murdered or was missing. His body, alive or dead, was never found.

Most criminal investigations in the early part of the century were dignified and leisurely. Villains took their time, they took trains and ships. In 1910, Dr. Crippen's arrest on board a liner, through the use of a radio-phone (while he was reading *The Four Just Men*), was thought by the public to be in bad taste. But there was something about the Ambrose Small case that created a feeling of open season. It was an opportunity for complaint about the state of the world; Small's blatant capitalism had clarified the gulf between the rich and the starving.

For the first year after Small's disappearance the public watched the police try to solve the case. But when they failed, and when the family put up an $80,000 reward for the millionaire's whereabouts, the public shouldered itself into the case. Now everyone looked for him. By 1921, one could be hired by a company at $4 a week as a 'searcher' and these individuals roamed the city and the smaller towns dragging suspicious strangers into police stations and having their measurements taken under the Bertillon process. The searchers resembled the press gangs of earlier centuries, and there were many rival organizations at work, investing in the project as if it were an oil field or a gold mine.

In 1924, after working for a year at various jobs in Toronto, Patrick Lewis became a searcher. The organizations were still active. It did not matter that five years had passed. No body had been found to fit Small's Bertillon chart and hordes of the otherwise unemployed were being hired. In these hard times any hope of a 'gusher' or 'strike' was worth pursuing. The search had turned the millionaire's body into a rare coin, a piece of financial property.

What held most interest for Patrick was the collection of letters the police had handed over to the family. Gradually he came into contact with Small's two sisters, who until then had found no one to take the letters seriously. Cranks, mediums, blackmail threats, the claims of kidnappers – the police and Small's wife had scorned them all. Patrick was befriended by the sisters at their house on Isabella Street. Clara Dickens knew him best, they told him. She was the rare lover. Talk to Briffa, said the sisters, he also thought she was the perfect woman for Ambrose – not Theresa, the wife, the *saint*.

Patrick took the train to Paris, Ontario, and met the radio actress Clara Dickens. She stood in the hall beside her mother and said she would not speak about Ambrose Small. She claimed not to have seen him since he disappeared. He stood there watching her. She asked him to leave.

In the books he read, women were rescued from runaway horses, from frozen pond accidents. Clara Dickens stood on the edge of the world of wealth. When she spoke to him she had been bending to one side as she attached an earring, gazing into the hall mirror, dismissing him, their eyes catching in the reflection. He was dazzled by her – her long white arms, the faint hair on the back of her neck – as if she without turning had fired a gun over her shoulder and mortally wounded him. The 'rare lover,' the 'perfect woman.'

And what else was she, apart from being the lover of Ambrose Small? Dressed up, about to go out, she had looked like a damsel fly, the sequins and gauze up to her neck. But there was something about the way she stood there, not turning around to talk to him properly.

When he went back the next morning she opened the door, her sleeves rolled up, those arms covered with flour up to her elbows.

– I thought you were rich, he said.

– Why? Do you want me to hire you to find my
beloved?

All that evening and late into the morning hours Patrick tried to
seduce Clara Dickens and then the next day when he was
exhausted she seduced him. He was reading through the old
news clippings about Ambrose in the Paris library when Clara
arrived. He was almost asleep over the 1919 files, his cheek
awkward on his shoulder as if someone had come up to him in
the silence of the reading room and broken his neck. She
strolled into the library dressed in white and stood in front of
the bookshelves.

– I'll drive you back to the Arlington Hotel.

Her voice wakened him. She turned a chair around so she
could straddle it and she leaned forward, her elbows against its
back. In her white dress she seemed the focus of all sunlight in
the library. There was laughter and then tenseness on her face.
Her long arm reached forward and picked up a clipping.

– You think I am the line to him, don't you? You think
that he must have left his shadow on me.

He couldn't talk back against her beauty. He noticed a fragment of water under her eyelid, a sun tear she was unaware of.

– Come. I'll drive you back to the hotel.

At that hour he did not think of seduction. He was exhausted
by all their conversations the previous night on her porch over-
looking Broadway Street. They had been outrageous and
flamboyant in each other's company, their arguments like
duets. He normally took months to approach someone, and at
the slightest rejection he would turn and never go back. But he

argued just so they could remain together on that porch deep in moonlight, half-laughing at the other's ploys. She wouldn't let him kiss her or hold her standing up – didn't want all of their bodies touching, that possibility.

They had walked in rain beside the Grand River towards her car. A gift from Ambrose, no doubt, he thought to himself. He was so tired there was no sophistication or cunning in him that night. And she herself did not know how to deal with this sudden obsession for her. She had driven him slowly back to the Arlington Hotel and they sat in the car.

     – Tomorrow the library for me, he said.
     – I could come and join you.

She clicked her tongue and jerked her head to the side suggestively.

It was two in the morning. She sat half-facing him, her feet already out of their shoes, one knee pointed towards him by the gear-shift. She let him kiss her goodnight and he sat there for a moment gazing at her face patterned by streetlight.

He got out and closed the door too energetically and realized after he had taken three steps how that had sounded. He turned back.

     – That wasn't a slam.
     – I know.

She was sitting there very alone, still, looking towards the seat he had left, her head down.

     – Goodnight.
     – Goodnight, Patrick.

Now they stepped from the news library into bright sunlight and they got into her car, Patrick carrying his cardboard box of notes. Both of them were so tired they hardly spoke during the drive back to the hotel.

His room when they got there was full of bright daylight and traffic noises came through the open window. They slept almost immediately, holding each other's hands.

When he woke, her eyes were studying him. Only her dark neck and face were visible. He felt awkward, having slept in his clothes.

    – Hello.
    – Sing to me, she murmured.
    – What?
    – I want it formal. Can you sing?

She smiled and he moved across the bed to her softness.

After they had made love he brought his pillow as close as he could for comfortable focus and gazed at her. When he woke she was gone, there was no answer on her telephone. He came back to the bed and inhaled whatever perfume there was left on the pillow.

*   *   *

    – Patrick, is that you?
    – Yes, Clara.
    – Doesn't sound like you.
    – I was asleep.
    – I'm taking you somewhere. Pick up some booze.
And a corkscrew. I've got the food. We should be away a few days.

It was a winding road they drove on towards Paris Plains, past gorges and tobacco fields.

— We're going to my friend's farmhouse.

— Ambrose?

— No, her name is Alice. I'll tell you about her later.

— You've got all the time in the damn world now.

— Later.

They entered a small farmhouse which had a woodstove in the kitchen. Bird feathers had been prised under the edges of wallpaper, here and there. In the front room there was a bed in an alcove, windows on three sides of it. A mat on the floor. There was hardly any furniture. It looked to him like the quarters of a monk. The friend was not to arrive for a couple of days, Clara said.

Later that night they lay on the bed by the three windows, barely dressed. He liked to sleep separate, in his own world, but with her he kept waking, reaching to hold her flesh against him. During the night Clara turned slowly like something on the floor of the ocean. She would put more and more clothes on in the darkness. She was always cold at night, in this room of the sea.

— You awake?

— What time is it? she said.

— Still night.

— Ahh.

— I love you. Were you ever in love? Apart from Ambrose.

— Yeah.

He was put off by her casual admission.

— I fell in love with a guy named Stump Jones when I was sixteen.

— Stump!

– There was a problem with the name.

– I'll say.

– Goodnight, Patrick, I'm sleepy.

– Hey!

He got up and strolled around the farmhouse happier and more at ease than he had ever been. She was already back in deep sleep, snoring, wearing one of his shirts to keep warm. A smile on her face. Clara the smirker. He wanted to get hold of Stump Jones and beat the hell out of him. Sixteen! Where had he been at sixteen? She had been Small's lover, Stump's lover, and who else? He found himself at this hour in the spell of her body, within the complex architecture of her past.

He had been looking through the window for over ten minutes when he suddenly focused on a shadow on the glass and saw it was a tree frog. He lit the oil lamp and held it up to the creature. A *pseudacris triseriata*. Hello friend, he breathed towards the pale-green speckled body hanging against the pane.

– Clara . . .

– What is it?

– Ambrose.

Love was like childhood for him. It opened him up, he was silly and relaxed.

– What!

She was wide awake, watching him as if he were crazy.

– Come here, I want you to see this.

She looked at the window and then back at him, refusing to speak.

– He wants you with all your clothes off.

– It's three in the morning, Patrick, you're supposed to

be asleep. You're supposed to be searching for my beloved. (*Beloved!* He grinned.) Do you want to make love, is that it?

– It's a tree frog!

– A tree frog in the moonlight is not rare.

– Yes it is, they only come out during the day. He wants to consider your thorax, your abdomen.

– Is this some kind of Bolshevik gesture?

She unbuttoned the shirt, stood between him and the glass.

– Tomorrow night he'll probably bring his pals to see you. Some places call them bell frogs. When they get excited they make a sound like a bell. Sometimes they bark like dogs.

She leaned forward and put her mouth to the green belly against the glass and kissed it.

– Hello Ambrose, she whispered, how are you doing?

Patrick put his arms around her and held her breasts.

– Marry me, willya . . .

He started barking.

– One of these days, soon, I'll go.

– To join Ambrose.

– Yes . . . I know he's alive.

– I have a fear I won't see you again.

– You talk on, Patrick, but you have no remorse.

– A strange word. It suggests a turning around on yourself.

– Don't speak. Here . . .

He met Ambrose in a dream. At the door he said, "There is this grey figure attached to my body, Patrick. I want you to cut it off me." They were old friends. All Patrick had was a penknife. He unfolded the blade and made Ambrose move into the hall, underneath the one light near the iron elevators. It was easier to see what it was now. A grey peacock had been sewn onto his friend. Patrick began to cut it away.

Ambrose was quiet. There appeared to be no pain at all. Patrick got down to the ankles and with a final saw from the knife the surplus figure curled off. It lay there like excess undercarpeting that had not been cleared away. They walked back to Small's door, shook hands, and parted. As he was falling through the final buildings of his dream he heard the news of Small's murder – he had been found vertically sliced in two.

– What?
– I said, were you dreaming?
– I don't know. Why?
– You were twitching.
– Hmmm. What kind of twitching?
– You know, like a dog asleep in front of the fire.
– Maybe I was chasing a rabbit.

They were sitting on the floor leaning into the corner of the room, her mouth on his nipple, her hand moving his cock slowly. An intricate science, his whole body imprisoned there, a ship in a bottle. I'm going to come. Come in my mouth. Moving forward, his fingers pulling back her hair like torn silk, he ejaculated, disappearing into her. She crooked her finger,

68

motioning, and he bent down and put his mouth on hers. He took it, the white character, and they passed it back and forth between them till it no longer existed, till they didn't know who had him like a lost planet somewhere in the body.

The next day they drove along the country roads in her Packard. He watched her as she spoke of the Wheeler Needle Works where her father had worked, the Medusa factory by the railway.

> – This is the tour of my teenage life, Patrick. I'll show you where I almost got seduced.
> – The crucial years.
> – Yes.

He loved the eroticism of her history, the knowledge of where she sat in schoolrooms, her favourite brand of pencil at the age of nine. Details flooded his heart. Clara said once, "When I know a man well socially, the only way I'll ever get to know him better will be to sleep with him." Seduction was the natural progression of curiosity. And during these days he found he had become interested only in her, her childhood, her radio work, this landscape in which she had grown up. He no longer wanted Small, he wanted to exorcise Small from Clara's mind.

It was raining and they couldn't get out of the car. She rolled down the window.

> – This is where I used to bury my lunch.

Taking his pocket handkerchief, she wet a corner with her tongue.

– You've got mud on you, she said, rubbing his forehead.

All these gestures removed place, country, everything. He felt he had to come back to the world.

– Tell me something about Ambrose quickly.
– Whenever he lied his voice became quiet and reasonable.
– What else.
– We used to fuck on the *Cayuga*.
– The day ferry? Jesus, on the *Cayuga*?

He was drawing out her history with Small, a splinter from a lady's palm. He was constantly appalled.

– Would it be forgivable to say I stayed with him because he gave me a piano?
– What are you telling me?
– I loved the piano. It was something to get lost in. My exit, my privacy. He had his money, gambling, he had his winning elsewhere. I had my radio work and my piano. Everyone has to scratch on walls somewhere or they go crazy. And you?
– I don't know.
– There was a time when I could have slept with his friend Briffa, for instance. Around him the air was always fraught with possibilities.
– I like fraught air.
– Briffa was lovely. European courtesy, a suggestion of brutality, happily married. I liked him because he was shaved down and focused. He decorated theatres. He had his vision, and that of course is a great aphrodisiac. The only man I met who had a vision. Ambrose

didn't. But he drew people like Briffa and others around him. Nobody else would touch them, let alone give them jobs. It was a battle – Small and his friends against the rest. Ambrose was laying siege, attacking all those remnants of wealthy families who really were the end of the line.

– And you were the pianist.

– Yes, the pianist, the musical interlude, the romance in the afternoon.

– He was the first to bugger me.

Patrick lay shocked and still beside her in the afternoon sunlight. When he spoke of his own past he was not calm like her. He flashed over previous relationships, often in bad humour. He would disclose the truth of his past only if interrogated with a specific question. He defended himself for most of the time with a habit of vagueness.

There was a wall in him that no one reached. Not even Clara, though she assumed it had deformed him. A tiny stone swallowed years back that had grown with him and which he carried around because he could not shed it. His motive for hiding it had probably extinguished itself years earlier. . . . Patrick and his small unimportant stone. It had entered him at the wrong time in his life. Then it had been a flint of terror. He could have easily turned aside at the age of seven or twenty, and just spat it out and kept on walking, and forgotten it by the next street corner.

So we are built.

– Who are your friends, Patrick?

– You. Only you.

– Alice comes tomorrow.

– We should go then.

– No, we can stay. You'll like her. But sometime after that I'll leave you.

– For Ambrose.

– Yes, for Ambrose. And you must never follow me.

– It takes me a long time to forgive.

– Don't worry, Patrick. Things fill in. People are replaced.

He wondered if at first she had been something he wanted to steal, not because she was Clara but because she belonged to the enemy. But now there was her character. This daughter of the foreman at Wheeler Needle Works, who seemed to have entered him like a spirit, bullying his private nature. She had been the lover of Ambrose Small, had been caught in the slow discreet wheel of the rich. And she would have learned those subtle rules that came alongside their gifts.

She started laughing, the hair on her temples still wet after their lovemaking. He sensed suddenly the sweat on himself as well. As he held her, he still didn't know who she was.

After midnight Clara strolls behind her friend Alice, removes the shawl from her shoulders, and ties it on as a headband. Patrick watches Clara intently – the bones, the planes of lamplight on her face, hair no longer in the way. Follow me, she could say in her shawl headband, and he would be one of the Gadarene swine.

– Did I tell you, Clara laughs, how I helped my father shave dogs? A true story. My father loved to hunt. He had four redbone hounds, with no names – they disappeared so often we used numbers. During the summer, hunters steal dogs and my father was always worried about theft. So we'd drive to the worst barber in Paris and ask him to clip the dogs. He was always insulted by this, though he had not much other business. I'd sit in the barber chair and hold the dog in my lap while it got clipped, and then we drove back with naked dogs. At home my dad got out his cow razor. He'd shave the midriffs to the skin, then we'd hose them and leave them to dry in the sun. After lunch my father wrote out DICKENS 1, DICKENS 2, and DICKENS 3 with tree paint in neat letters on their sides. I was allowed to paint the name on the last dog. We had to hold them to the ground until the paint dried properly. I wrote DICKENS 4.

Those were favourite times. All day we'd talk about things I was not sure of. About plants, what wine tasted like. He put me right on how to have babies. I thought I had to take a watermelon seed, put it between two pieces of bread and drink lots of water. I thought this was how my parents talked when they were alone. We'd chat to the dogs too who were nonplussed, looking thin and naked. Sometimes it seemed to me I'd just had four babies. Great times. Then my father died of a stroke when I was fifteen. Dammit.

– Yeah, says Patrick, my father too. . . . My father was a wizard, he could blow logs right out of the water.

– What happened?

– He got killed setting charges in a feldspar mine. The company had tried to go too deep and the section above him collapsed. There wasn't an explosion. The shelf just slid down with him into the cave and drowned him. He was buried in feldspar. I didn't even know what it was. They use it in everything – chinaware, tiles, pottery, inlaid table tops, even in artificial teeth. I lost him there.

– Here's to holy fathers, Alice says, holding up her glass.

Conversation dips again into childhood but the friend Alice plucks only details from the present to celebrate. She reveals no past, remains sourceless, like those statues of men with wrapped heads who symbolize undiscovered rivers.

All night as they talk the sky and the fields outside seem potent with summer storm. The night kitchen with these two actresses is overwhelming. Clara and Alice slip into tongues, impersonate people, and keep each other talking long into the night. Patrick is suddenly an audience. They imitate the way men smoke. They discuss how women laugh – from the raucous to the sullen to the mercenary. He is in a room full of diverse laughter, looking back and forth from Clara's vividness and erotic movement, even when she stretches, to Alice's paleness and suppressed energy. "My pale friend," Clara had called her.

At three in the morning there is thunder in the distance. Patrick cannot keep his eyes open. He says goodnight, and abandons himself to the sofa, closing the door to the kitchen.

The two women continue talking and laughing, a glance of sheet lightning miles away. After an hour or so they say to each other, "Let's get him."

In the darkness of the farmhouse Clara and Alice approach his bed. They carry candles and a large roll of paper, whispering to each other. They uncover the face of Patrick hidden in the green blanket. This is enough. The candles are placed on a straight-back chair. They cut the paper with draper's scissors and pin the four corners of it to the floor. They begin to draw hard and quickly, as if copying down a blueprint in a foreign country. It seems as illicit as that. Approaching a sleeping man to see what he will reveal of himself in his portrait at this time of the night.

He sleeps, and during the next while they work together on the same sheet which sometimes tears with the force of the crayon. They have done this often to each other, these spirit paintings, the head leaking purple or yellow – auras of jealousy and desire. Given the vagueness of his covered body, they draw upon all they know or can guess about him. They kneel, their heads bright beside the candlelight, crayoning against the texture of the floor. Anger, honesty, stumble out. One travels along a descant of insight and the other follows, completes the phrase, making the gesture safe.

75

A cave mural. The yellow light flickers upon his face against the sofa cushion, upon the two women sweating during this close night, their heads down as if pulling something out of a river. One leans back to stretch while the other explores the portrait. "Are we witches?" Alice asks.

Clara begins to laugh. She moans like a spirit looking for the keyhole out of the room. She places her hands on the frail walls, then her mouth explodes with noise and she tugs Alice out into the Ontario night. They crash down the wood steps, Clara's growls unnaming things, their bodies rolling among the low moon flowers and grass and then leaping up as the rain breaks free of the locked heat clouds, running into the thunder of a dark field, through the stomach-high beans and corn, the damp rustle of it against their skirts and outstretched arms – the house fever slipping away from them.

The rain comes through their thin cotton clothes against their muscles. Alice sweeps back her wet hair. A sudden flinging of sheet lightning and Clara sees Alice subliminal in movement almost rising up into the air, shirt removed, so her body can meet the rain, the rest of her ascent lost to darkness till the next brief flutter of light when they hold a birch tree in their clasped hands, lean back and swing within the rain.

They crawl delirious together in the blackness. There is no moon. There is the moon flower in its small power of accuracy, like a compass pointing to where the moon is, so they can bay towards its absence.

*   *   *

He moves quietly through the house in the early morning. At the top of the stairs he looks through a small round window into the fields. This is a fragile farmhouse. He has felt the winds shake it during the night. Now there is a strange peace, grass and trees seen through the white light of morning, the two women asleep. Yesterday they were up at dawn flinging rhubarb across the room at each other – as he discovered, waking to riotous laughter. He found them in the midst of battle, Alice bent over in laughter, in tears, and Clara suddenly sheepish when she saw him enter the kitchen.

Now there is no noise but the creak of his moving. In the bedroom he finds them asleep in each other's arms, unaware of daylight filling the room. He touches the elbow of Alice Gull and her flesh shifts away. He puts his hand into her palm and she grips it unconsciously, not fully awake.

- Hi.
- I have to go soon, he says. A train.
- Ummm. We left you a present from last night.
- Yes?
- She'll explain it later.

She stretches carefully without disturbing Clara.

- Throw me a shirt, I'll have breakfast with you.

In the kitchen Patrick cuts open a grapefruit and hands her half. Alice shakes her head. She remains sitting on the stool in the long pink shirt and watches him move, efficient in her kitchen. He slides through company, she notices, as anonymously as possible. She points to certain drawers silently when he asks for spoons or a spatula.

Patrick is not a breakfast talker and in fifteen minutes he is ready to leave. She holds his arm at the door. He kisses her accidentally too close to the eye.

– Give her a kiss for me.
– I will.
– Tell her I'll see her tonight at the hotel.
– Okay.

She closes the door firmly and watches him through the window on his walk to the train station, striding from one frame of glass to another.

She climbs back into bed with Clara, puts her arm around her to accept the warmth she has lost by rising. Welcomes the sleepy haven of Monday morning.

His mind remains against them, like an impress of his hand on their sleeping flesh, the cold train window at his cheek. Hungry for Clara, he thinks about Alice as if he has not focused on her before, as if Alice being touched by Clara has grown magically, fully formed.

*   *   *

In the Arlington Hotel that night he studies the large drawing Clara has tacked to the door. He has come off well, Clara tells him, the soul is pliable. He does not believe her. Unless his soul expands during sleep, unless sleep somehow attaches the disparate elements of his character. Perhaps the portrait will teach him. He loves the closeness between the two women and he enjoys their gift of his supposedly guardless nature.

– What did you think of her?
– I liked her.
– She's a great actress.
– On the radio?

– No, on the stage.

– Better than you, is she?

– By a hundred miles.

– Yes, I liked her.

Later he will think of the seconds when he was almost asleep and they entered the dark room with candles. The approach of magicians. He feels more community remembering this than anything in his life. Patrick and the two women. A study for the New World. Judith and Holofernes. St. Jerome and the Lion. Patrick and the Two Women. He loves the tableau, even though being asleep he had not witnessed the ceremony.

Sometimes when he is alone Patrick will blindfold himself and move around a room, slowly at first, then faster until he is immaculate and magical in it. He will parade, turn suddenly away from lampshades, duck under hanging plants, even run across the room and leap in his darkness over small tables.

All night long Patrick and Clara have talked, the name of Ambrose like a drip of water in their conversation. All night they have talked about her plan to join her 'beloved,' the sound of his name like a poison, like the word *nicotine*. She will leave tomorrow. She will not tell him where Small is. She demands that he not try to follow her after they drive to Toronto to put her on the train. Patrick feels he knows nothing of most of Clara's life. He keeps finding and losing parts of her, as if opening a drawer to discover another mask.

They sit half-dressed on the bed on this last morning. All night long they have talked and he has felt inarticulate against the power of his unseen enemy, unable to persuade Clara out of this journey towards Ambrose. He offers to perform his trick for her, draws her long silk shawl from the sleeve of her coat, doubles it, and ties it around his eyes.

He positions Clara on the bed and tells her not to move. Then he takes off into the room – at first using his hands for security, then ignoring them, just throwing his body within an inch of the window, swooping his head down parallel to shelves while he rushes across the room in straight lines, in curves, as if he has the mechanism of a bat in his human blood. He leaps across the bed delighted at her shriek. He is magnificent. He is perfect, she thinks.

He mutters to her as he moves – "Watch this tray" – as he flings it up and catches it. "And this eggshell on the floor which I'll crush like the bones of Stump Jones. You are so beautiful, Clara, I'll never go blind. I want to go to sleep gazing at your face each night. I couldn't be satisfied with just touching you, smelling you." He throws an apple into her lap, rips the date off the calendar. "I practised some nights when you were asleep." He leans forward and bites the apple, chewing and talking.

She refuses all this and moves off the bed, positioning herself on the northeast corner of the rug. She puts her palms against her ears to stop hearing his endearments and stands there with her elbows sticking out. He is moving, almost frantic, now yelling his love. She can still hear him, and presses her palms tighter against the sides of her head, and closes her eyes. She feels the floor shudder under her, feels she is surrounded, contained by his whirling. Suddenly she is hit hard and her left hand jars against her skull, knocking her over.

She gets to her knees, dazed, and looks around. Patrick is grabbing a part of the sheet towards his face. He is snuffling, blood begins to come out of his nose onto the sheet. The blindfold is around his neck like a collar. He looks up at her and, as if he can't see her, turns back to the sheet as he continues to bleed.

— You moved. I told you not to. You moved.

She still cannot stand up from the pain and the dizziness. She knows if she tries to stand she will fall over again. So she sits where she is. Patrick is bent over watching the sheet in his hands.

So much for the human element, he thinks.

All his life Patrick Lewis has lived beside novels and their clear stories. Authors accompanying their heroes clarified motives. World events raised characters from destitution. The books would conclude with all wills rectified and all romances solvent. Even the spurned lover accepted the fact that the conflict had ended.

After Clara leaves him, Patrick cleans his room on Queen Street obsessively. Soap crystals fizz in a pail, the mop slices the week's dust. Then he sits in the only dry corner where he has previously placed cigarettes and smokes the Roxy, dropping ash into the bucket beside him. The room smells like a clean butcher shop. The furniture – a table, a chair, and an iguana cage – is piled on the bed at the street end of the room.

Sometimes he leaves a book in this corner. He has already smelled the pages, touched the print's indentations. Now he can devour it like a loaf of bread with his bare hands. He wipes cigarette ash off his arm and opens *Wild Geese*. "*It was not openly spoken of, but the family was waiting for Caleb Gare. Even Lind Archer, the new school teacher, who had come late that afternoon all the way from Yellow Post with the Indian mail carrier and must therefore be hungry, was waiting.*" Clara wiping his forehead with her handkerchief. "*The rocker seemed to say, 'Caleb! Caleb! Caleb!' It amused the Teacher, rather wanly.*" Her ear listening to the skin that covered Patrick's heart.

He feeds the iguana, holding the vetch an inch from the neutral mouth. Only the eyelid sliding down changes its expression. An animal born of another planet. He strokes the jaw with the flower. Through the window he sees men appear in the blue Toronto sky, inching into the air, scaffolding it. Pieces of Clara float around him.

A kiss at Union Station, her mouth half-open.

> – I'm sorry to ask you but I can't take it across the country. Will you keep him?
> – What is this, a door prize?
> – Don't talk like that, Patrick.
> – Let it free, dammit.
> – It's blind!

Stumbling back from argument.

> – Feed it clover and vetch, lots of water. Rattle the cage before you put food in. Just to let him know.

So he had watched Clara climb, prim, silver-buckled, into the train. He walked home with the cage banging against his knee, threw in a cabbage, and left the animal alone for a week. It heard his tirades, the broken cups and glasses. The iguana knew Clara Dickens, knowledge of her was there within its medieval body. Patrick believed in archaic words like *befall* and *doomed*. The doom of Patrick Lewis. The doom of Ambrose Small. The words suggested spells and visions, a choreography of fate. A long time ago he had been told never to follow her. If Patrick was a hero he could come down on Small like an arrow. He could lead an iguana on a silver leash to its mistress.

Dear Clara

All these strange half-lit lives. Rosedale like an aquarium
at night. Underwater trees. You in a long black dress
walking without shoes in Ambrose's long garden while his
wife slept upstairs. Howling up to disturb her night. The
soft rich.

Ambrose had class because he had you. That's what they
all knew – those half-formed people who were born with
money and who did nothing except keep it like a
thermometer up their ass. The mean rich. The soft rich. I
know why you went with Ambrose. He was the harbour
rat. An immigrant rat. He had to win or he lost everything.
The others just had to get their oldest son into Upper
Canada College. Crop rotation. The only one who could
slide over the wall, skip along the broken glass, was Small.
But I don't want Small, I want you. . . .

Dear Clara

All night the tense and bitter conversations of lovers
after they exit from the Greenwood bar across the street
from my room. I lie by the window for summer air, and
late-night couples assuming privacy seduce or accuse or
fight. *No I didn't. I'm sorry. Goddamn you!* Whispered.
The slap, the blow of scorned love, the nails of the other in
their rake across his eyes. This battle for territory, Clara,
ownership and want, the fast breath of a fuck, human or cat
– supernatural moans, moon talk – her hands over the face
making him less anonymous, the back of her coat against
brick. *You were telling him something, what were you
telling him? Damn you! What! Nothing!*

I keep waking to sudden intimacy. Once I heard a strange
humming below and looked out. A man with a carpet
draped over his shoulder accompanied by a red dog. It was

the neighbourhood thief, Caravaggio, returning from work. He passed calmly under me, absorbed in the eating of Sicilian ice cream. . . .

I woke to your voice in danger. You were whispering. I thought at first it was dialogue from the street but it was you and I froze in the darkness – a possible dream I did not wish to let slip. I know your hesitations, your cracking voice when you are lying or getting drunk. These are familiar to me. Clara? I said into the darkness, it's okay, it's okay. I was standing on the mattress at the foot of the bed. I could have touched the ceiling with both hands. But you didn't listen. I was aware of wind coming in off the street. A male voice laughed in your company. I turned and saw the lit cream-yellow of the radio dial. It was Mystery Hour, a replay from two or three years back. I had slept through hours of broadcasting and woke only to the pitch of your breaking voice. You had a bit part. In the plot you had fallen on bad times.

At Union Station I refused to leave you. Your face angry against the Bedford limestone, *Damn you, Patrick, leave me alone!* Your hair crashes against it as you gesture and break free of me.

At Gate 5 you stop, pause in the steam, putting your hands up in surrender like a cowboy. A truce. No we did not walk up those steps, our fingers locked like cogs. You were escaping the claustrophobia an obsessed lover brings. We placed our arms on each other's shoulders, panting. Your face poured its look out.

Dear Clara

I came up to you and asked for a dance. The man with you punched me in the face. I asked you once more and he punched me in the face. I wiped off the blood below my eye. Five minutes later I came back to your table and his men attacked me, leaving me in a back alley. In this dream I hadn't seen you for a long time and I loved you in your dress. It was a big celebration of some sort, you were with honourable company. I would be looking at your face and a hand would hit me. I would fall to the floor. I'd be lying there looking at your dress, then dragged away. I finally came back and asked you to dance. Two things happened. For a brief while we were dancing. I wanted to hold you close but I did not want to get blood on you and you said, "It's all right, Patrick," and then I was watching your face as they began forcing me back to the alley. The dream ended with me plotting with the Chinese to break up the party.

*　　*　　*

He opened the door to her and stepped back quickly, appalled. He had not expected her.

He walked into the empty rooms, gesturing towards the broken things he was trying to assemble, broken glass and crockery, things he had flung long ago, after Clara had gone.

> – What are those things?
> – Glass, a crossword puzzle . . . a story.

Alice grinned at him. How much did she know about him and Clara anyway?

> – I'm trying to get my life in order, he said.
> – Well, this should begin it.

She moved around the room, touching nothing, as if everything in the sparse living room were potent and part of his cure.

86

– How long has she been gone? A year and a half?
Two years?
  – Longer. Not long enough.

He spoke in bursts. Sentences needed additions, parentheses, to clarify not the information but his state.

  – Give me a coffee, Patrick.

There was more than five feet between them. When she moved closer towards a news clipping attached to the wall, he automatically moved further back. He felt dangerous. Alice seemed older, confident. She removed her coat and laid it on the ground by the door. He followed her into the kitchen, pumped water into the saucepan for coffee, and lit the gas. There were no chairs so she sat on the counter opposite, watching him at the stove. She was safe there.

  – You look tired, she said.
  – Oh, I'm okay. Physically I'm fine, just my mind. I'm lucky, whatever state I'm in my body takes care of itself.

It was his longest speech for months.

  – I'm the reverse. That's the only way I can tell if I'm in bad shape mentally, through my body.
  – Well, you're an actress, right?
  – That's right.

His eyes were on everything but her, a bad sign. She slid off the counter and approached him, then stopped, inches away. His eyes caught hers, moved away, and then settled safely on her cheek.

  – The next move, Patrick.

His first smile for months. He leaned forward and clung to

her to stop her vanishing. She was smaller than he imagined. She wasn't thin, or very small, but he had thought her body against him would be a different size. He could see the red in her hair by the temples, the lines under her eyes.

The water in the saucepan was boiling and they did not move. They stood together feeling each other's spines, each other's hair at the back of the neck. Relax, she said, and he wanted to collapse against her, be carried by her into foreign countries, into the ocean, into bed, anywhere. He had been alone too long. This was a time when returning from work he would fall nightly into a cave of dreams, so later he was not sure it happened. It had been sudden, nothing was played out to conclusion, nothing solved by their time together, but it somehow kept him alive. She had come that day, he thought later, not for passion, but to save him, to veer him to some reality. If anyone knew where Clara was, she did.

He had almost walked past Alice the previous week, outside the Parrot Theatre. He had not seen her since the farmhouse near Paris Plains, two years earlier, and he had hardly recognized her. But she had yelled his name.

> – Were you at the play?
> – No . . .

He shrugged distractedly. His face and eyes were wild, were seeing nothing on the street around him. His clothes old, unironed, the collar bent up.

> – What are you doing now? she asked.

He moved himself away from her extended arm.

> – I'm working at a lumber yard.
> – Come and see the play some night. Meet me afterwards.

– Yes, all right.

The 'yes' was so he could get away. He had wanted to shake her to pieces, blame her for Clara. It seemed it was all a game of theatre the two of them had performed against him. A woman's education, removing his cleverness, even his revenge. He had turned and walked away from her.

Now, taking Alice's smallest finger, he walked with her from the kitchen.

> – How long have you lived here?
> – Almost a year.
> – There's just a bed!
> – There's an iguana.
> – Oh *you've* got him.

In bed her nature, her transparency, had startled him. As did her sudden animal growl onto his shoulder when she lay on top of him. They lay there in the blank room.

> – I think her mother knows where she is, Patrick.
> – Possibly.
> – You should look for her.
> – She told me not to.
> – You must remove her shadow from you.
> – I know that.
> – Then when we meet again we can talk . . . we can
> say hello.

She said that so strangely he would later recall it differently – clothed in sarcasm or tentative love or sadness.

She had lost an earring when she got up. She said it didn't matter, that it was artificial.

He went to see Clara's mother in Paris and had a late dinner with her.

> – When she married she eloped. But that didn't last long.
> – She *married* Stump Jones?
> – And divorced him. Anyway, too many people laughed at his name. It was a terrible thing to live with and he would not change it. She was only eighteen. He said he'd gotten used to it.
> – What was he like?
> – Stump was good-looking and bad-tempered. It was the snickering over hotel registers that got to her. Patrick Lewis, now, that's a *brick* of a name. She told me a good deal about you.
> – What did she say?
> – That you were probably a romantic Bolshevik from southern Ontario.
> – Well, I'm an eastern Ontario boy. Go on.
> – She said she seduced you.
> – She said *that* . . . she said things like *that* to you?
> – Yes.
> – Did she ever keep in touch with Stump?
> – I don't think so.
> – Do you have a photograph of them?

Mrs. Dickens got up from the sofa and went into the kitchen. He thought she was angry, felt him rude, so he followed her and started apologizing.

– Forget her, Patrick, it's been over two years.

He laughed.

She pulled open the cupboard drawer and handed him the honeymoon photograph. Both of them against some damn rocks. Stump looked okay, but it was her face he kept gazing at. So young, her hair almost blonde then, not dark as it was now. A fuller face, innocent.

> – It's a foolish face, he said, not quite believing it was the same person.
> – Yes, said her mother, she was foolish then.
> – Where is she?
> – I don't like him.
> – Nobody does. Do you know where she is?
> – In a place Small knows you will never look . . . in a place he knows you will never go back to.
> – What do you mean?

But he knew then. Knew exactly where they were. He had been the searcher who had gazed across maps and seen every name except the one which was so well-known it had remained, like his childhood, invisible to him.

*   *   *

Patrick stares at the thin layer of moonlight on the wall. His body feels like the shadow of someone in chains. He had awakened once to Clara whispering at the foot of his bed in this Paris hotel room. Soaking wet. Two in the morning. She'd slid the buttons through the damp holes of her dress . . . and another time crawled from their bed to warm her hands on the radiator. . . . He undreams himself, remembers she has left him.

Gets out of bed and walks to the wall beside the radiator against which she had leaned.

He is standing in their old room at the Arlington Hotel. Without turning on any light he bends down and puts his face close to the wall at stomach level. Here they had pushed in frenzy, sexual madness. He finds the faint impression of her backbone on the white paint.

Ambrose Small holds a wooden match above his head, its glare falling onto the shoulders of his nightshirt. Four in the morning. Above him a silk bag holds naphtha. He has heard noises. His other hand turns a brass handle. Now the flame and gas combine and his room breaks open in yellow light. Patrick Lewis is sitting in an armchair, overcoat on, looking straight at him.

Small draws up a chair. A mutual excitement, as if each were looking into a mirror.

      – Where do you want me to begin, says Small, with my childhood?

Patrick smiles.

      – I don't want to talk about you, Small. I want Clara. Something about her cast a spell on me. . . . I don't know what it is.
      – It's her unfinished nature, Ambrose says quietly.
      – Perhaps.
      – Who else knows I am here?
      – No one. I came just to talk to her.
      – I'll wake Clara. Go outside, she'll come out and listen to you.

Patrick steps outside into the dark night and sits in one of the two chairs on the grass. He is among blue trees, he can smell gum on the branches. He can hear the river. He knows this place from his childhood, the large house belonging to the Rathbun Timber Company, which he had passed every day during the log drives. A last remnant from that era. He walks to the window and looks in. There is no longer light. Ambrose must have carried the lamp back into the bedroom of the house.

Water from the eaves dribbles onto Patrick's coat, some on his neck, and he steps back, stretching in the darkness. But there had been no rain. He notices a metal smell. He moves his eyes above the ledge of the window and simultaneously knows it has nothing to do with rain. He smells and feels kerosene pour across his shoulders, hears the rasp of the match that will kill him in the hand of Small who crouches on the roof. Patrick sees it fall like a knighthood towards his shoulders.

He is running along the rock path to the river before he knows for certain he is on fire. His hand pulls the knife out of his pocket and uses it to slice open the coat as he runs. He stops and begins to laugh. He is all right. Then he sees light in the trees around him and knows he is a hunchback of fire, and he runs – past the barrel for burning garbage, past the boat on the sand – and falls stomach down in the shallows, splashing forward. The air caught in his coat is a bubble on fire burning above the water. He turns and falls onto his back.

He remains in the water, only his head visible, scared to allow his shoulders into the air. There is no pain except in his hands, which still hold on to the knife. He sticks it into the river bottom. Patrick can feel the cuts in his palm. He can feel the itch on his chest from slashing open the coat.

He looks past his hand just in time. Ambrose is standing on the beach. The bottle with the burning-cloth neck is travelling

94

in the air and the explosion when it hits the water makes the river around him jump like a basket of fish, makes the night silver. Patrick's left eye goes linen white, and he knows he is possibly blind there. He reaches for the knife and stumbles out, wading free of the water. Ambrose hasn't moved. He doesn't move as Patrick steps up to him and cuts him at the shoulder.

Then Patrick is running towards the old hotel in the village of Bellrock, a mile away. He does not trust himself to use shortcuts over the fields so he stays with the road, running past the house he was born in, over the bridge he had fished off, and up the stairs into the hotel room.

When Patrick woke, he could still not see properly out of one eye. His wet clothes were bunched on a chair in front of the small grate. Now and then he would get up, wrap the thin quilt around his chest, and sit by the window looking down at the river. The same river, downstream from Small's house, Depot Creek, scarred where the loggers tore open the banks to build dams. Some kids were fishing knee-deep by the dock. He sat at the window feeling the leak of air through the glass. His hands stiff on his lap seemed to be someone else's hands that he was looking at in a picture. He heard Clara's voice on the other side of the door.

He saw his ghost in the mirror. He pushed back the bolt with his shoulder, the quilt like a cape over him.

– Turn the handle, I can't do that.

As she came in, he moved his hands out of the way, the paws of a boxer. It hurt to put them down at his side.

– Oh god it *is* you.
– Hello, Clara.

She stood there, her coat open, her hands in her pockets. She was taking in what he looked like. His face was wet and he realized his damaged eye was crying, he was unable to control it. If you can't see you can't control anything, he thought. Patrick had imagined her so often when she had not been wearing these clothes. He lifted his left arm up to wipe his face with the quilt but when his arm got to the level of his shoulder it began to shake. She came forward and wiped his cheek with her open hand, then put the wet hand of salt to her mouth.

– I can't see out of this eye.

Her hand came up to his face again, her fingers feeling his skin, the flesh on his cheek.

– Can you feel that?
– Yes.

Her fingers moved into his scalp. He didn't know where to put his hands. He couldn't get them out of the way.

– What's wrong?
– My hands.
– Put them around me, we *have* touched before.
– I don't want you to think . . .

He grinned and his face ached. They stood then like that in the room. His hands on either side of the rough material of her coat, her fingers gently parting his hair to feel his scalp.

– There's blood here. What the hell were you two doing?

She moved out of his hold and shrugged off her coat.

– I know a doctor in town, but I'll clean you up first.

Patrick stood at the window looking out. She came up behind him.

– I've imagined us meeting all over the world, Patrick, but I never thought we'd meet here. By this river you told me about.

She put her head against him and they were still, as if asleep. Her finger traced a delicate line down along his shoulder, parallel to a cut.

– It would be terrible if we met under perfect conditions. Don't you think?

With a bowl of hot water beside her, she worked the dried blood out of his hair. He was tired and fought to stay awake. She squeezed the cloth dry and started washing his cuts, the one on his chest, his shoulder, and then finally his hands, getting him to gradually move his stiff fingers.

– Do you have your shaving stuff? Yes, you must.

She touched the menthol pencil to three cuts in front of his ear, then suggested that she shave him. She rinsed the razor and sat in front of him, straddling the chair.

– How are you, Patrick?

He gave his nervous laugh that she loved.

– I'm on the verge as usual.
– Don't lose that.

He looked directly into her eyes, aiming himself at her. The first time he had looked at her continually. There wasn't any pain in his face, she noticed, just thirst.

— Talk to me, Clara.
— All these small scars . . .

She wiped the razor on the quilt. He looked older. More brittle. This was the way to know somebody's face, she thought. She should have shaved him before. She should have understood his breakable quality sooner. He was a creature of habit, he belonged with the last century. She wanted to paint his face, to follow the lines of his cheek and eyebrow with colours. Make another spirit painting of him. He was less neutral now, his skin like the texture of a cave that would transform anything painted on it. She lathered his face, wanting to sculpt him. With her finger she wrote DICKENS 5 on his forehead. "I don't want you lost, Patrick. I can't have you but I don't want you to get lost."

She stepped bowlegged off the chair and stretched her body to break the cramp, moving backwards until she was leaning against the wallpaper. Then she walked to the window. She saw him gazing straight ahead towards the wallpaper, as if she had left her body there. Flowers, vines, now and then an English pheasant in the foliage, now and then a rip caused by a drunk logger in other times trying to get out of the room, unable to find the door. He sat looking at that landscape in front of him.

— Do you know this area had a Small sighting? It made the Toronto papers and I knew it was no coincidence. He had to be living in the town I came from because *you* were with him. He grilled you the way I did. Isn't that right?

– He wanted to know where you came from. I didn't tell him much. He wasn't interested in you, Patrick. He's a rich man who escaped from a rich shoe. He protects himself. He will never believe it was me you came after.

He turned his head and watched her face on the pillow looking up at the ceiling.

– In a way I knew I'd be injured when I saw you again. I had dreams about coming up to you at dances and being beaten back.

She leaned over and touched his chest.

– The doctor put on a good dressing.
– Does Small know you're here with me?
– Probably, but don't talk about him, Patrick. I'll go back in the morning.

When she looked at his face a short while later he was asleep. The medication had made him drowsy all evening. She kept watching him a long time. Around three in the morning she felt his body against her. They touched, both moving careful of his wounds, all over each other as if meeting in a dream. Later she made her way to the bathroom and came back in a silhouette. He was comfortable and tired.

– Goodnight, Clara.
– Goodnight, Patrick Lewis. My friend.

He slept gripping her hand.

She dressed in the darkness and left without waking him. The sun came up over Goose Island, hitting the tin roof of Mr. Moir's house as she walked home, past the Grants and the Meeks. She saw young George Grant with his brother Russell coming back with the cows and they spoke for a few minutes. She continued to the bend in the road and down the curling path to the house they lived in and would probably move from now. She felt somehow deliriously happy between the two points of this journey.

When she reached the house she didn't go in but went down to the beach and sat facing the water, leaning against the red boat. It was cold but she had her coat on and she was thinking. Not knowing what was happening now at the hotel, that with the light Patrick had awakened to find the sheets thick with blood which had escaped from his dressings, from their moving together in the darkness, discovering even the print of her hand perfect on the wallpaper, a print of blood on the English flowers of his bedroom where she had leaned to balance herself in their lovemaking as she crouched over him. The dressings hung off him like a limp white rib while Ambrose came down from the house and saw her sitting there thinking, looking at Patrick's river.

2

PALACE OF PURIFICATION

IN THE TUNNEL under Lake Ontario two men shake hands on an incline of mud. Beside them a pickaxe and a lamp, their dirt-streaked faces pivoting to look towards the camera. For a moment, while the film receives the image, everything is still, the other tunnel workers silent. Then Arthur Goss, the city photographer, packs up his tripod and glass plates, unhooks the cord of lights that creates a vista of open tunnel behind the two men, walks with his equipment the fifty yards to the ladder, and climbs out into sunlight.

Work continues. The grunt into hard clay. The wet slap. Men burning rock and shattering it wherever they come across it. Filling hundreds of barrels with liquid mud and hauling them out of the tunnel. In the east end of the city a tunnel is being built out under the lake in order to lay intake pipes for the new waterworks.

It is 1930. The cut of the shovel into clay is all Patrick sees digging into the brown slippery darkness. He feels the whole continent in front of him. They dig underneath one of the largest lakes in North America beside a hissing lamp, racing with the speed of their shadows. Each blow against the shale wall jars up from the palms into the shoulders as if the body is hit. Exhaustion overpowers Patrick and the other tunnellers within twenty minutes, the arms itching, the chest dry. Then an hour more, then another four hours till lunch, when they have thirty minutes to eat.

During the eight-hour shifts no one speaks. Patrick is as silent as the Italians and Greeks towards the *bronco* foremen. For eight hours a day the air around them rolls in its dirty light. From somewhere else in the tunnel there is the permanent drone of pumps attempting to suck out the water, which is constantly at their heels. All morning they slip in the wet clay unable to stand properly, pissing where they work, eating where someone else left shit.

As the muckers move forward with their picks and shovels, the gunnite crew sprays a mixture of concrete and sand onto the walls, which would otherwise crumble after a few hours of exposure to the air. And if they are digging incorrectly – just one degree up, burrowing too close to the weight of Lake Ontario during this mad scheme by Commissioner Harris to collect lake water 3,300 yards out in the lake? They have all imagined the water heaving in, shouldering them aside in a fast death.

Whenever the tunnellers reach large walls of rock or shale beds the foreman clears the tunnel and the transportation mules are herded back. Then Patrick separates himself from the others. He removes his belt that has the buckle, pats his wet clothes for any other sign of metal, and hoists the box of dynamite onto his shoulder. With a lamp he walks towards the far reaches of the tunnel alone. There is no sound here – no wind, no noise of work. He hears only the slosh of his feet tromping through water, his own breathing in the darkness.

At the end of the tunnel he holds the lamp up against the dark wall, trying to imagine the structure of the rock in front of him, the shape, its possible fissures. He puts the lamp down and augers out holes for the sticks of dynamite. Only at these times are his eyes close to what he digs into all day. The burn of the lamp spills against the wet earth as he works. Once it revealed the pale history of a fossil, a cone-shaped cephalopod, which he sheared free and dropped into his pocket.

Although he dynamites for the foreman, most of the time Patrick works with the muckers in the manual digging. He is paid extra for each of the charges laid. Nobody else wants the claustrophobic uncertainty of this work, but for Patrick this part is the only ease in this terrible place where he feels banished from the world. He carries out the old skill he learned from his father – although then it had been in sunlight, in rivers, logs tumbling over themselves slowly in the air.

He sidewinds the powder fuse, which will burn at two minutes to the yard, and ignites it. He picks up the lamp and begins his walk back to the others. There is no hurry, there is no other light in the tunnel but this one lamp and as he moves his shadow shifts like a giant alongside him. When he reaches the others at the shaft he hears with them the crumple of noise as the shale displaces and the rock splinters into shards and flints in the far darkness under the lake.

As the day progresses heat rises in the tunnel. The men remove their shirts and hammer them into the hard walls with spikes. Patrick can recognize other tunnellers on the way home by the ragged hole in the back of their shirts. It is a code among them, like the path of a familiar thick bullet in the left shoulder blade. At the end of the day they climb from the tunnel into the desert of construction which had been Victoria Park Forest, where the waterworks is now being built. They see each other's bodies steaming in the air.

Patrick embraces the last of the light on the walk home. In

the dry air the clay hardens on clothing, whitens his arms and hair. He takes a knife and cuts free the mud between his boots and trouser cuffs, brushes the blade over the laces to loosen them. In his Wyatt Avenue room he drops all his clothes in a corner, feeds the iguana, and crawls into bed. He picks the clothes up again at six in the morning hard as armour and bangs them against the wall of the fire escape till they crack apart and soften, the dust in the air around him. At the Thompson Grill he eats breakfast in ten minutes. He reads no paper, just watches the hands of the waitress break open the eggs. As he goes underground the humidity will fall back into his clothes quick as rain.

Carrying three lanterns, the crew of nine men walks towards the end of the tunnel. Already they can smell each other and the sweat from the previous days, the lamp wick raised to burn out odour. They can hear the mules and pit-horses who live down here, transporting the dug earth and mud barrels to the ladder. When these creatures were lowered down the shaft by rope they had brayed madly, thinking they were being buried alive. Patrick and the others walk silently, remembering the teeth of the animals distinct, that screaming, the feet bound so they wouldn't slash out and break themselves, lowered forty feet down and remaining there until they died or the tunnel reached the selected mark under the lake. And when would that be? The brain of the mule no more and no less knowledgeable than the body of a man who dug into a clay wall in front of him.

Above ground, like the blossoming of a tree, the excavations and construction were also being orchestrated. The giant centrifugal pumps, more valuable than life, were trolleyed into place with their shell-shaped impellers that in Commissioner Harris' dream would fan the water up towards the settling basins. Cranes lowered 800 tons of steel sheet piling rolled in Sault Ste. Marie. Trucks were driving in the bricks from Cooksville.

From across the province the subcontractors brought in their products and talents to build a palace for water. Richie Cut Stone Company, Raymond Concrete, Heather & Little Roofing and Sheet Metal, ornamental iron from Architectural Bronze and Iron Works, steel sashes from Canadian Metal Window and Steel Works, elevators from Otis-Fenson and Turnbull, glazing from Hobbs Glass, plasterers from Strauss & Scott, overhead doors from the Richard Wilcox Canadian Company. The Bavington Brothers sent painters, Bennett and Wright were responsible for heat and ventilation, the linoleum came from T. Eaton Company, the mastic flooring from Vulcan Asphalt. Mazes of electricity were laid down by Canadian Comstock, Alexander Murray composed the floor design. The tiling and terrazzo were by Italian Mosaic and Tile Company.

Harris had dreamed the marble walls, the copper-banded roofs. He pulled down Victoria Park Forest and the essential temple swept up in its place, built on the slope towards the lake. The architect Pomphrey modelled its entrance on a Byzantine city gate, and the inside of the building would be an image of the ideal city. The brass railings curved up three flights like an immaculate fiction. The subtle splay on the tower gave it an Egyptian feel. Harris could *smell* the place before it was there, knew every image of it as well as his arms – west wing, east wing. The Depression and the public outcry would slow it all down, but in spite of that half of it would be completed within a year. "The form of a city changes faster than the heart of a mortal," Harris liked to remind his critics, quoting Baudelaire.

He was providing jobs as he had in the building of the Bloor Street Viaduct, the St. Clair Reservoir, the men hired daily for grading, clearing bush, removing stumps, and rip-rapping the sides of streams. The Commissioner would slide these facts out, bounce them off his arms like oranges to journalists.

But Harris was building it for himself. For a stray dream he'd always had about water, water they should have taken across the Bloor Street Viaduct as he proposed. No one else was interested in water at this time. Harris imagined a palace for it. He wanted the best ornamental iron. He wanted a brass elevator to lead from the service building to the filter building where you could step out across rose-coloured marble. The neo-Byzantine style allowed him to blend in all the technical elements. The friezes depicted stylized impellers. He wanted herringbone tiles imported from Siena, art deco clocks and pump signals, unfloored high windows which would look over filter pools four feet deep, languid, reflective as medieval water gardens.

But first he needed to finish the spear of tunnel a mile out under the lake and organize the human digging and the human and mule dragging of pipes all the way out there for the intake of water. This was the other tentacle of his dream. The one that reached out and clung to him in a nightmare where faces peered out, working in that permanent rain of condensation.

He had sent Goss and his photographers down but he had not entered the tunnels himself. He was a man who understood the continuity of the city, the daily consumptions of water, the speed of raw water through a filter bed, the journeys of chlorine and sulphur-dioxide to the island filtration plant, the 119 inspections by tugboats each year of the various sewer outfalls, and the approximate number of valves and caissons of the East Toronto pumping stations, and the two miles a year of water-main construction – from the St. Clair Reservoir to the high-level pumping station, and the construction of the John Street surge tank. . . .

This was choreography in 1930.

In those photographs moisture in the tunnel appears white. There is a foreman's white shirt, there is white lye daubed onto rock to be dynamited. And all else is labour and darkness. Ash-grey faces. An unfinished world. The men work in the equivalent of the fallout of a candle. They are in the foresection of the cortex, in the small world of Rowland Harris' dream as he lies in bed on Neville Park Boulevard.

Such a strange dream for him. The silence of men coming out of a hole each within an envelope of steam. Horses under Lake Ontario. Swallowing the water one-and-a-quarter miles away, bringing it back into his body, and spitting it out clean.

*   *   *

Patrick ate most of his meals at the Thompson Grill on River Street where the waitress, through years of habit, had reduced to a minimum the action of pouring coffee or flipping an egg. He could spot the oil burns on her wrists, the permanent grimace in her eye from the smoke.

If she looked at those who ate here it occurred when they were not aware of it. She seemed self-sufficient, something underwater in the false yellow light of the narrow room against the street, the flawed glass creating shadows in the air. There was something transient about her though she had been there for years. Most of the chewers at the Thompson Grill had that quality.

Patrick would sit at an uncleared section so he could watch

the fingers of her left hand pluck up the glasses and cups while the other hand, the muscles in intricate movement under the skin, swabbed the counter clean. It was several months before he became aware of the tattoo high on her arm, seeing it through a tear in the seam where the cotton had loosened.

He came to believe she had the powers of a goddess who could condemn or bless. She would be able to transform the one she touched, the one she gripped at the wrist with her tough hand, the muscles stiffening up towards the blue-black of the half-revealed creature that pivoted on the bone of her shoulder. His eyes wanted to glimpse nothing else.

He pinned the note, saying *Waterworks – Sunday 8 p.m.* to the wall above his bed in case he forgot, though it had been his only invitation in two years. "The cheese stands alone," he'd sing to himself, while buying groceries along Eastern Avenue. Patrick loved that song. He found himself muttering "The farmer takes the dog . . . the farmer takes the dog" among the Macedonians, as if perfecting a password. The southeastern section of the city where he now lived was made up mostly of immigrants and he walked everywhere not hearing any language he knew, deliriously anonymous. The people on the street, the Macedonians and Bulgarians, were his only mirror. He worked in the tunnels with them.

He had discovered the Macedonian word for iguana, *gooshter*, and finally used it to explain his requests each evening at the fruit stall for clover and vetch. It was a breakthrough. The woman gazed at him, corrected his pronunciation, and yelled it to the next stall. She came around the crates and outlined the shape of a lizard. *Gooshter?* Four women and a couple of men then circled him trying desperately to leap over the code of languages between them. His obsession with vetch had puzzled them. He had gone at one point into the centre of the city, bought some, and returned to the Macedonians to show them what he needed. The following week, a store owner had waved it to him as he came down Eastern Avenue. Vetch was *fee-ee*. But now they were onto serious things. A living creature, a *gooshter*, had been translated. He was surrounded. They were trying to discover how many he had. Was raising them one of his professions? They knew where he lived, of course, had seen his yellow light looking down on Wyatt Avenue, knew he was alone, knew down to the very can of peaches what he ate in a week. Peaches on Friday. They had sent someone to find Emil, who spoke the best English, and when the boy arrived he said, "Peaches on Friday, right?"

Patrick felt ashamed they could discover so little about him. He had reduced himself almost to nothing. He would walk home at dusk after working in the lake tunnel. His radio was on past midnight. He did nothing else that he could think of. They approved of his Finnish suit. *Po modata eleganten!* which meant stylish! stylish! He was handed a Macedonian cake. And suddenly Patrick, surrounded by friendship, concern, was smiling, feeling the tears on his face falling towards his stern Macedonian-style moustache. Elena, the great Elena who had sold him vetch for over a year, unpinned the white scarf around her neck and passed it to him. He looked up and saw the men and women who could not know *why* he wept now among these strangers who in the past had seemed to him like dark blinds on his street, their street, for he was their alien.

And then he had to remember new names. Suddenly formal, beginning with Elena. The women shook his hand, the men embraced and kissed him, and each time he said Patrick.

Patrick. Patrick. Knowing he must now remember every single person. And now, because it was noon, the King Street Russian Mission Brass Band fifty yards down the road, they invited him to lunch which was set up on tables beside the stalls and crates. He was guest of honour. Elena on one side of him, Emil on the other, and a table of new friends.

He was brought a plate of cabbage rolls – *sarmi*, Elena said, and suddenly the awful sulphurous odour he had smelled for the last year since moving was explained. Emil was describing the technique of soaking cabbage leaves in a solution of salt and water and a bit of vinegar and leaving it there for days. Patrick ate everything that was put in front of him. During coffee, Kosta, the owner of the Ohrida Lake Restaurant, sent along a question to Emil. Emil asked two or three others first to see if this question was apt. Then he turned to Patrick. "What else can you do?" The table was silent. Elena put her hand on his and sent a qualifier via Emil. "It does not matter if you don't do anything." The others down the table nodded.

– I used to be a searcher. I can work dynamite.

Emil's translation created an even greater silence. Patrick could hear every note of the Russian Mission Band down the street. Then Kosta jumped up and yelled something at Patrick. His face looked at him with anger, full of passion. Emil turned to Patrick now, having to yell above the sudden din at the table. "He says 'Me too, me too.'" Kosta grabbed a round loaf of bread, leapt free of the bench, and booted it down the road in the direction of the Russian Mission Band.

Later that afternoon when Patrick was showing the iguana to the street, the man Kosta said, "The waterworks at eight, Sunday night. A gathering." Then he drifted away, not allowing Patrick to reply or question the invitation.

An hour after dusk disappeared into the earth the people came in silence, in small and large families, up the slope towards the half-built waterworks. Emerging from darkness, mothlike, walking towards the thin rectangle of the building's southern doorway. The movement was quickly over, the wave of bodies had seemed a shadow of a cloud over the slope.

Inside the building they moved in noise and light. It was an illegal gathering of various nationalities and the noise of machines camouflaged their activity from whoever might have been passing along Queen Street a hundred yards away. Many languages were being spoken, and Patrick followed the crowd to the seats that were set up around a temporary stage. He saw Kosta, who was busy greeting and shepherding people, and he watched him until Kosta caught his eye. Patrick waved and Kosta raised his hand and continued with what he was doing. Patrick felt utterly alone in this laughing crowd that traded information back and forth, held children on their laps.

The four-piece band was playing by the stage. It was a party and a political meeting, all of them trespassing, waiting now for speeches and entertainment. Patrick found a seat and took a sip from his flask. Almost immediately the electric lights were turned off, leaving only the glow from oil lamps on the edge of the platform.

The puppets arrived on stage in a mob, their wooden bones clattering. The semicircle of oil lamps cast yellow onto this section of the pumping station – onto the generators, the first few rows of the audience, the mosaic tiles, and brass banisters. Patrick looked up and saw the grid above them on the upper level, hardly visible, where the puppeteers must have been lying in darkness.

The forty puppets moved into the light, their paws gesturing at the air. The males had moustaches and beards, the females had been given rouged faces. There was one life-sized puppet. This giant in their midst was the central character in the story, its face brightly coloured: green-shadowed eyes and a racoon ring of yellow around them so they were like targets. All of the puppets looked stunned. Feet tested air before each exaggerated step was taken on this dangerous new country of the stage. Their costumes were a blend of several nations. It was five minutes into the dance before Patrick realized that the large puppet was human. And this was only because the dancer moved out of his puppet movements and began to twirl in gestures impossible for wood.

The large figure began to distinguish itself from the others. It became a hero not by size but by gesture and the detail of character. Perhaps it was an exceptional puppet of cloth as opposed to an exceptional human being. Behind the curled moustache it was perturbed and nervous – ambitious, scared, at times greedy. It varied its emotions from fear to desire. The other puppets included a prune-faced rich woman, a policeman, the sly friend, the family matriarch. The hero linked them all. There was no noise, no drum-beat or song. Just the clattering of their feet, just the wooden hands touching each other gently the way fingernails touch glass. The puppets ranged all over the stage or huddled together as a chorus, warning the hero of his ambition, gesturing him down with laws. The human puppet, alien and naive and gregarious, upset everything. The face, in spite of the moustache, was dark and young. He wore a Finnish shirt and Serbian pants.

A plot grew. Laughing like a fool he was brought before the authorities, unable to speak their language. He stood there assaulted by insults. His face was frozen. The others began to pummel him but not a word emerged – just a damaged gaze in the context of those flailing arms. He fell to the floor pleading with gestures. The scene was endless. Patrick wanted to rip the painted face off. The caricature of a culture. His eyes could not move away from that face.

The audience around him was silent. The only sounds on stage were grunts of authority. They were all waiting for the large puppet to speak, but it could say nothing. The thick eyebrows, the big nose, the curled moustache – all of which parodied them – became haunting. When the figure wheeled now the sweat on the pink brocade shirt made it blood-red along the spine and shoulders. It stamped a foot to try and bring out a language. The other puppets shifted like bamboo to the side of the stage. The figure knelt, one hand banging down on the wooden floor as if pleading for help – a terrible loudness entering the silent performance.

The audience began to clap in unison with the banging hand, the high hall of the waterworks echoing. Patrick was unable to move, his eyes locked upon the crouched figure, the manic hand. If it was not stopped it would burst. That was absurd. He wanted the hall to be quiet, the figure's terror stopped. He could see the yellow-ringed eyes, the shirt bloody from the darkness of sweat, the mask of the painted face looking up like a dog. Patrick stood up and stumbled over feet until he reached the aisle. He wanted to be out of here, out of this building. He was covered in the heartbeat of applause which started to come faster. Each footstep as he moved released the terrible noise. He was among members of the band, the silent band which sat there waiting for the next act when they would be required to play. He saw the huge instruments on their laps, which in their curls and convolutions looked like frozen organs of the body. He climbed up, slipping at first because he still couldn't remove his eyes from the face and the banging white hand. He stepped over a lamp. Then he was up there on stage, and as soon as he approached the exhausted figure he saw up close that the performer was much smaller, that it was a woman.

He knelt and held her by the shoulders, his arm on her damp back. He leaned forward, caught the hand still trying to smash down again like a machine locked in habit, a swimmer unable to stop. He swerved the palm away from the floor and brought it slowly down to her thigh. Then he looked up, through the halo of light into the sudden silence.

There was a crowd standing on the upper level as well. Hundreds more than he had thought. He looked back at the woman, the costume made of false silk, a cheap glittering material from the streets, drenched in sweat. This close he could recognize nothing of the figure he had seen perform. It seemed washed out, exhausted statuary. One tear of sweat cut a path through the thick makeup. Now the eyes, hidden in the circles of paint, focused on him, then reacted with shock. She bent forward. He felt his hand slide against the sweat of her cheek. He had forgotten where he was. She pulled herself up, her arm on his shoulder. She walked downstage slowly towards the kerosene lights, spreading her hands wide and then clapping them. A slow beat. There. There. There.

Then, with her arms out, the crowd cheering, she raised her swollen hand and now everyone was standing yelling at her.

She brought her fingers to her lips and the audience became quiet. She threw the name of the next performer into their midst like a bell, and a man walked into the light carrying an umbrella. The crowd was immediately with him. Patrick began to move backwards to the makeshift curtain. He looked down embarrassed and when he looked up again she had left the stage.

Backstage he would be an outsider. He recalled the touch of that hand on his shoulder as she pulled herself up. And the voice he had recognized. He tried to remember the washed-out face, its features under the makeup. Behind the curtain there were just a few performers in half-light – one kerosene lamp on the floor. How should he enter a room where a giant takes off its head? Where a dwarf stands up to full height. The Macedonian juggler he had watched perform half an hour earlier with absolute abandon was packing the thirty hard oranges neatly into his suitcase. No sofas, or arches of light, just performers cleaning up. A man putting on his socks. Someone reading *The Racing News*. At the far end of the hall he saw an Indian walking a puppet towards a corridor, as if escorting someone frail. Patrick went after him. The man turned right along the Venturi corridor and disappeared behind another curtain. Here among the strangely shaped pipes and meters the air was humid. A great cheer went up from the audience. As the man came out Patrick caught his arm and asked him where the puppet dancer was. The Indian jerked his head towards the curtain and handed him a flashlight.

He walked into pitch darkness. When he turned on the flashlight he saw swaying feet. He moved the light up the brocade robe – a king hung up there, the strings and wood handle attached to a pipe. Three or four ceiling pipes held all of the puppets in mid-air. He swung the amber beam from side to side, and everywhere he turned, the light picked out faces and arms that no longer looked like puppets but relaxed humans, a shadow conference. It was a king's court, silent – a custom of the East. Whenever the royal gong struck, the court of the Moghul prince Akbar remained frozen at whatever they were doing. It was the whim of a monarch during which time he moved among his retainers and subjects to study their dress and activity. Movement meant execution. He walked into kitchens, armouries, bedrooms where lovers would lie frozen on the verge of touching, walked past dining-tables where the court sat hungry or bored looking at the cooling food, stepped into the quarters of falconers where only the birds moved and fussed on their perches.

So Patrick moved in this darkness, the eye of the flashlight swallowing the colours, the room turning under his gaze like a jewel. What had been theatrical seemed locked within metamorphosis. He wanted to put his hand up and unbutton a blouse, remove a shoe. He moved quickly towards a figure but it was only a queen draped over a chair, sitting the way a queen would sit. He heard the cheers from the hall once more.

Patrick switched off the light and stood there. His eyes remembering scarlet, the puff of a blue sleeve, the flat brown feet pathetic as a peacock's under such grand costuming. A broken ochre hand. A *splash*. He turned to face the sound.

He moved forward, one hand in front of him to hold away the costumed bodies, lifting his feet up high so he would not trip in the darkness. He thought, I am moving like a puppet. He touched an arm in the darkness not fully realizing it was human. A hand came from somewhere and held his wrist. "Hello, Patrick." He turned on the flashlight. She was waiting for the light, like a good actress, ready to be revealed.

"No one is allowed here while I wash. I knew it had to be you. . . ." She was wearing a singlet and had been washing herself from a bowl, her hands now squeezing out a cloth in the basin and wiping her face, streaks of flesh across the paint. One line of colour remained that seemed to show her frowning. Behind her a puppet slowly pivoted. He could smell the candle she must have blown out as soon as she heard him enter. "You can help with the paint on my neck."

Patrick did not speak. The light moved down her arm to the bowl, illuminated her hand which wet the cloth, squeezed it, and moved forward to give it to him. She saw his right hand reach to take it from her. His hand began to wipe her neck. He removed the brown paint, turned her around and slowly wiped the vermilion frown-mark by her mouth, the light close on her face.

He rinsed out the cloth again and holding her forehead steady wiped the targets off her eyes, cloth over one finger for precision, the blue left iris wavering at the closeness . . . so that it was not Alice Gull but something more intimate – an eye muscle having to trust a fingertip to remove that quarter-inch of bright yellow around her sight.

They were now many hours into the night. In her room on Verral Avenue. He had just seen the sleeping child.

  – I wasn't married, she said. Her father is dead. He was like a *comitidjiis*. A *chetnik*. Do you know what that means?

He shook his head continuing to look out the window into the rain. He felt there was space in her small rooms only when he looked out.

  – Open it, Patrick. If it's raining the cat will want to come in. They are national guerrillas. Political activists. Freedom-fighters in Bulgaria and Turkey and Serbia. They were tortured, then some of them came here. They have a very high level of justice.

She smiled, then continued.

  – They are very difficult to live with.
  – I think I have a passive sense of justice.
  – I've noticed. Like water, you can be easily harnessed, Patrick. That's dangerous.
  – I don't think so. I don't believe the language of politics, but I'll protect the friends I have. It's all I can handle.

She sat on the mattress looking up at him, the cat purring in her lap as she dried it with a towel.

— That's not enough, Patrick. We're in a thunderstorm.
— Is that a line from one of your tracts?
— No, it's a metaphor. You reach people through metaphor. It's what I reached you with earlier tonight in the performance.
— You appealed to my sense of compassion.
— Compassion forgives too much. You could forgive the worst man. You forgive him and nothing changes.
— You can teach him, make him aware . . .
— Why leave the power in his hands?

There was no reply from him. He turned away from her, back to the open window and the rain.

— You believe in solitude, Patrick, in retreat. You can afford to be romantic because you are self-sufficient.
— Yes, I've got about ten bucks to my name.
— I'm not talking about money. Working in the tunnels is terrible, I know that. But you have a choice, what of the others who don't?
— Such as.
— Such as this kid. Such as three-quarters of the population of Upper America. They can't afford your choices, your *languor*.
— They could succeed. Look at —
— Come on, Patrick, of course some make it. They do it by becoming just like the ones they want to overtake. Like Ambrose. Look at what he became before he disappeared. He was *predatory*. He let nothing cling to him, not even Clara. I always liked you because you

123

knew that. Because you hated that in him.

   – I hated him because I wanted what he had.

   – I don't think so. You don't want power. You were born to be a younger brother.

She stood up now and began pacing. She needed to move her arms, be more forceful.

   – Anyway, we're not interested in Ambrose any more. To hell with him, he's damned.

The power of the girl's father was still in her. Patrick couldn't tell how much of a role it was. She spoke slowly now.

   – There is more compassion in my desire for truth than in your 'image' of compassion. You must name the enemy.

   – And if he is your friend?

   – *I'm* your friend. Hana there sleeping is your friend. The people tonight in the audience were your friends. They're compassionate too. Listen, they are terrible sentimentalists. They love your damn iguana. They'll cry all through their sister's wedding. They'll cry when their sister says she has had her first kiss. But they must turn and kill the animals in the slaughter-houses. And the smell of the tanning factories goes into their noses and lungs and stays there for life. They never get the smell off their bodies. Do you know the smell? You can bet the rich don't know it. It brutalizes. It's like sleeping with the enemy. It clung to Hana's father. They get skin burns from the galvanizing process. Arthritis, rheum-atism. *That's* the truth.

   – So what do you do?

   – You name the enemy and destroy their power. Start

with their luxuries – their select clubs, their summer mansions.

Alice stopped pacing, put a hand up to the low slope of the ceiling and pushed against it.

– The grand cause, Patrick.

He knows he will never forget a word or a gesture of hers tonight, in this doll-house of a room. He sits on the bed looking up at the avid spirit of her.

– Someone always comes out of the audience to stop me, Patrick. This time it was you. My old pal.
– I don't think you will convert me.
– Yes. I can.
– If it was valuable to some cause for me to kill someone would you want me to do it?

She picked up the cat again.

– Would the girl's father have done that?
– I don't think I'm big enough to put someone in a position where they have to hurt another.

It had stopped raining. They climbed out onto the fire escape, Alice carrying the sleeping girl, the air free and light after the storm. She was smiling at the girl. He felt he was looking at another person.

– Hana is nine years old. Already too smart. Not enough a child, and that's sad.
– You've got a lot more time with her.
– No. I feel she's loaned to me. We're veiled in flesh. That's all.

They looked out over the low houses of Queen Street, the metal of the fire escape wet around them, cool, a shock to their arms on this summer night. The rain had released the smells from the street and lifted them up. He lay back like the child, a raindrop now and then touching his shirt like a heartbeat.

    – *I don't know*, she whispered, near him.

He reached to where she was and she put her hand against him. The sky looked mapped, gridded by the fire escape. Above and below them a few neighbours came out onto the frail structures, laughing with relief at the cooler air. They would wave now and then, formally, to Alice and her companion. He was suddenly aware that he had a role.

A bottle of fruit whiskey on the end of a long piece of twine swung from side to side in front of them. Alice caught it and pulled it in. "To impatience," she said. She drank, offered him some, and then holding the rope let the bottle down to another level. In this way it moved among the others.

To the south they could see the lights of the Victory Flour Mills. The Macedonians, who disliked the raindrops on their hair, asked their wives to pass them their hats through the window, and felt more secure. They saw Alice's man who worked in the tunnels. They sat among their families, looking towards the lake. The vista was Upper America, a New World. Landscape changed nothing but it brought rest, altered character as gradually as water on a stone. Patrick lay back again beside Alice and the girl Hana.

    – You should sit up, she said after a while. You will
  see something beautiful.

A rectangle of light went on below them. Then another. The night-shift workers were starting to get up. They could be seen in grey trousers and undershirts, washing at their kitchen sinks. The neighbourhood was soon speckled with light while the rest of the city lay in sleep. Soon they could hear doors closing on the street below them. Figures filed out, Macedonians and Greeks, heading for the killing floors and railway yards and bakeries.

— They don't want your revolution, Patrick said to Alice.
— No. They won't be involved. Just you. You're a mongrel, like me. Not like my daughter here. But like me.
— So what do you want?
— Nothing but thunder.

*   *   *

Alice and Hana were still on the fire escape, curled up together, when he left. He closed the door on them quiet as a thief.

He would have to go back to his room, take his clothes out into the alley and beat the hardened mud out of them, then walk to work. It was about five A.M., his head and body buzzing, overloaded with false energy. Later, he knew, he would be unable to lift his arms above his head, would stagger under the weight of a pickaxe. But for now the dawn in him, the sun, wakened his blood.

He remembered Clara in the Paris hotel talking about how Alice had been after the child's father had died. "Hana wasn't born yet. But Cato died and I think she went into madness, into something very alone. He was killed up north when she was pregnant."

In the Thompson Grill, the counter radio was already playing songs about the heart, songs about women who let their men go as casually as a river through their fingers. The waitress with the tattoo gave him his coffee. The music this morning threw him across eras. He was eighteen again and he fell into a girl's arms, drunk and full of awe during his first formal dance, painted moonlight on the ceiling, the floating lights through the scrims that bathed the couples translating them. He had stepped up cocky and drunk onto the sprung floor and was suddenly close enough to see the girl's lost eyes, undisguised by the colours, and he too was lost. A chameleon among the minds of women.

> – *What did you think of my friend?*
> – *I liked her.*
> – *She's a great actress.*
> – *Better than you, is she?*
> – *By a hundred miles, Patrick.*
> – *Yes, I liked her.*

His mind skates across old conversations. The past drifts into the air like an oasis and he watches himself within it. The girl's eyes that night when he was eighteen were like tunnels into kindness and lust and determination which he loved as much as her white stomach and her ochre face. He saw something there he would never fully reach – the way Clara dissolved and suddenly disappeared from him, or the way Alice came to him it seemed in a series of masks or painted faces, both of these women like the sea through a foreground of men.

These were days that really belonged to the moon.

He was restless and full of Alice Gull. When the tunnel at the waterworks was completed, Patrick got a job at Wickett and Craig's tannery. His flesh tightened in this new dry world, his damp stiffness fell away.

All day he thought of her as he cut skins in the Cypress Street leather factory. Jobs were still scarce and it was only through Alice's friends that he was hired. Patrick's shoulder nudged the bolster that released rolls of leather onto the floor and he waded into the brown skins with the pilot knife, slicing the hides in straight lines. When his line was finished he would stand breathing in the cold air till someone else came off the cutter's alley. He was no longer aware of the smell from the dyers' yards. Only if it rained would the odour assault his body.

He was one of three pilot men. Their knives weaved with the stride of their arms and they worked barefoot as if walking up a muddy river, slicing it up into tributaries. It was a skill that insisted on every part of the body's balance. Alice would smell the leather on him, even after he had bathed in the courtyards when work was over, the brief pelt of water and steam on the row of them standing on the cobblestones. They were allowed only ten seconds of water. The men who dyed the leather got longer but the smell on them was terrible and it never left.

Dye work took place in the courtyards next to the warehouse. Circular pools had been cut into the stone – into which the men leapt waist-deep within the reds and ochres and greens, leapt in embracing the skins of recently slaughtered animals. In the round wells four-foot in diameter they heaved and stomped, ensuring the dye went solidly into the pores of the skin that had been part of a live animal the previous day. And the men stepped out in colours up to their necks, pulling wet hides out after them so it appeared they had removed the skin from their own bodies. They had leapt into different colours as if into different countries.

What the dyers wanted, standing there together, the representatives from separate nations, was a cigarette. To stand during the five-minute break dressed in green talking to a man in yellow, and *smoke*. To take in the fresh energy of smoke and swallow it deep into their lungs, roll it around and breathe it up so it would remove with luck the acrid texture already deep within them, stuck within every corner of their flesh. A cigarette, a star beam through their flesh, would have been enough to purify them.

That is how Patrick would remember them later. Their bodies standing there tired, only the heads white. If he were an artist he would have painted them but that was false celebration. What did it mean in the end to look aesthetically plumaged on this October day in the east end of the city five hundred yards from Front Street? What would the painting tell? That they were twenty to thirty-five years old, were Macedonians mostly, though there were a few Poles and Lithuanians. That on average they had three or four sentences of English, that they had never read the *Mail and Empire* or *Saturday Night*. That during the day they ate standing up. That they had consumed the most evil smell in history, they were consuming it now, flesh death, which lies in the vacuum between flesh and skin, and even if they never stepped into this pit again – a year from now they would burp up that odour. That they would die of consumption and at present they did not know it. That in winter this picturesque yard of colour was even more beautiful, the thin layer of snowfall between the steaming wells. Below-zero weather and the almost naked men descend into the vats at the same whistle and cover themselves later with burlap as they stand waiting.

The only virtue to winter was the removal of smell. They did not want a cigarette then, they could hardly breathe. Their mouths sent forth plumes. They stood there, the steam coming through the burlap. And when they stopped steaming they knew they were too cold and had to go in. But during October, as Patrick watched them during his break from the hide-room, they desired a cigarette. And they could never smoke – the acid of the solutions they had stepped into and out of so strong that they would have ignited if a flame touched them.

A green man on fire.

They were the dyers. They were paid one dollar a day. Nobody could last in that job more than six months and only the desperate took it. There were other jobs such as water boys and hide-room labourers. In the open cloisters were the sausage and fertilizer makers. Here the men stood, ankle-deep in salt, filling casings, squeezing out shit and waste from animal intestines. In the further halls were the killing-floors where you moved among the bellowing cattle stunning them towards death with sledge hammers, the dead eyes still flickering while their skins were removed. There was never enough ventilation, and the coarse salt, like the acids in the dyeing section, left the men invisibly with tuberculosis and arthritis and rheumatism. All of these professions arrived in morning darkness and worked till six in the evening, the labour agent giving them all English names. Charlie Johnson, Nick Parker. They remembered the strange foreign syllables like a number.

For the dyers the one moment of superiority came in the showers at the end of the day. They stood under the hot pipes, not noticeably changing for two or three minutes – as if, like an actress unable to return to the real world from a role, they would be forever contained in that livid colour, only their brains free of it. And then the blue suddenly dropped off, the colour disrobed itself from the body, fell in one piece to their ankles, and they stepped out, in the erotica of being made free.

What remained in the dyers' skin was the odour that no woman in bed would ever lean towards. Alice lay beside Patrick's exhausted body, her tongue on his neck, recognizing the taste of him, knowing the dyers' wives would never taste or smell their husbands again in such a way; even if they removed all pigment and coarse salt crystal, the men would smell still of the angel they wrestled with in the well, in the pit. Incarnadine.

"I'll tell you about the rich," Alice would say. "The rich are always laughing. They keep saying the same things on their boats and lawns: *Isn't this grand! We're having a good time!* And whenever the rich get drunk and maudlin about humanity you have to listen for hours. But they keep you in the tunnels and stockyards. They do not toil or spin. Remember that . . . understand what they will always refuse to let go of. There are a hundred fences and lawns between the rich and you. You've got to know these things, Patrick, before you ever go near them – the way a dog before battling with cows rolls in the shit of the enemy."

In Kosta's house he relaxes as Alice speaks with her friends, slipping out of English and into Finnish or Macedonian. She knows she can be unconcerned with his lack of language, that he is happy. She converses with full energy in this theatre of the dinner table, her face vivid; a scar, a mole will exaggerate when not disguised by the content of conversation. He in fact pleasures in his own descant interpretations of what is being said. He catches only the names of streets, the name of Police Chief Draper, who has imposed laws against public meetings by foreigners. So if they speak this way in public, in *any* language other than English, they will be jailed. A rule of the city. The *broncos* will have them arrested as many already have been in various rallies in High Park or in the Shapiro Drug Store clash with the Mounties in the previous year.

He watches each of her friends and he gazes at the small memory painting of Europe on the wall – the spare landscape, the village imposed on it. He is immensely comfortable in this room. He remembers his father once passing the foreign loggers on First Lake Road and saying, *"They don't know where they are."* And now, in this neighbourhood intricate with history and ceremony, Patrick smiles to himself at the irony of reversals. Before the meal, Kosta's wife had come up to him, pointed to one of the pictures and named her village, then she had pressed the side of her stomach with both hands sensually to make clear to Patrick that she would be serving liver.

If only it were possible that in the instance something was written down – idea or emotion or musical phrase – it became known to others of the era. The rejected *Carmen* of 1875 turning so many into lovers of opera. And Verdi in the pouring rain believing he was being turned into a frog – even this emotion realized by his contemporaries.

Patrick listens now as Alice reads to him from the letters of

Joseph Conrad — an extract which she has copied. She has already asked him who he likes to read and he has mentioned Conrad. "Yes, but," she says rising as the child cries, "have you read his *letters*?" In the other room she comforts the girl Hana out of a nightmare.

"Wait," she continues, "I've got something to show you." Very excited now, as if she fears he will get up and leave before she can present this gift. She too likes Conrad. She likes his theatrical style. There are some novelists whose work actors love but who could not write a simple scene for the stage. They write the scenes actors dream, and Conrad was that for Alice.

> — Listen: "An idle and selfish class loves to see mischief being made, even if it is made at its own expense."
> — *Ha*, he laughs.
> — He's complaining about Tory views on Spanish liberal insurgents of the 1830s, based in London. "Of course I do not defend political crimes. It is repulsive to me by tradition, by sentiment, and even by reflection. But some of these men struggled for an idea, openly, in the light of day, and sacrificed to it all that to most men makes life worth living. Moreover a sweeping assertion is always wrong, since men are infinitely varied; and harsh words are useless because they cannot combat ideas. And the ideas (that live) should be combatted, not the men who die."

It was a letter Conrad had written to a newspaper. So Patrick listened to his contemporary.

– How can I convert you? she would ask in the darkness of the bedroom.

– The trouble with ideology, Alice, is that it hates the private. You must make it human.

– These are my favourite lines. I'll whisper them. "I have taught you that the sky in all its zones is mortal. . . . Let me now re-emphasize the extreme looseness of the structure of all objects."

In the darkness he can see just the faint aura of her hair.

– Say it again.

*   *   *

On Saturday afternoons the dye washers and cutters, men from the killing beds, the sausage makers, the electrocuters – all of them from this abattoir and tannery on Cypress Street – were free. After bathing under the pipes they walked up Bathurst Street to Queen, the thirty or so of them knowing little more than each other's false names or true countries. *Hey Italy!* They were in pairs or trios, each in their own language as the dyers had been in their own colours. After a beer they would continue up Bathurst to the Oak Leaf Steam Baths. Paying their quarters they were each handed a towel, a sheet, a padlock, and a canvas bag. They stripped, packed their clothes and salaries into the bag, locked it, and strung the keys around their necks. There was a sense of relaxation among all of them. *Hey Canada!* A wave to Patrick. It was Saturday.

In the whitewashed rooms they sat naked within the steam, brushing a scab, considering a scar on the shoulder. Someone he had never spoken to caught his eye and both of them were so tired they could not turn away their gaze, just watched the other bluntly. He knew nothing about the men around him except how they moved and laughed – on this side of language. He himself had kept his true name and voice from the bosses at the leather yard, never spoke to them or answered them. A chain was pulled that forced wet steam into the room so that their bodies were separated by whiteness coming up through the gridded floors, tattoos and hard muscles fading into unborn photographs. They shifted, stood up, someone began to sing.

The wet heat focused the exhaustion and under the cold shower the last of the tension fell to his feet. For the last hour they lay on the green bunks, a radio on the windowsill transmitting the Saturday afternoon opera, with a sign above it in three languages insisting that no one change the station.

He lay there, not wanting translation, letting the emotion of the music fall onto him. Soon this arm would become the arm Alice kissed. They were all being released from the week's work and began to allow themselves ease, the clarified world of passion. The music of *La Bohème*, the death of Mimi, hovering over their unprotected bodies, the keys hanging from the cords around their necks.

*　　*　　*

Then it was her hand in the doorway touching his heart, against his ribs, aware through her fingers of his weariness. In the small room where he could take three steps and touch the window. There was Patrick and Alice and Hana. If it was warm they would eat on the fire escape. Or if Alice was working he and Hana walked over to the Balkan Café where they sat on wire chairs and were served by long-aproned waiters. They ordered *bop* and *manja*, Hana telling him in her clear, exact voice what the names meant. *Bop* was beans. *Manja* was stew. As he watched Hana, her face drifted into Alice's and back again as if two glass negatives merged, then moved apart. It was not so much the features as the mannerisms of Alice that he witnessed in her daughter.

He was at ease with the precise Hana and the way she seriously articulated herself among strangers. That voice knew what it wanted and knew what it was allowed. He wanted to pick Hana up and embrace her on the street but felt shy, though in games or in a crowded streetcar her arm lay across him as if needing his warmth and closeness. As he did hers.

But his relationship with Alice had a horizon. She refused to speak of the past. Even her stories about Hana's father, though intricate, gave nothing away of herself. She was never self-centred in her mythologies. She would turn any compliment away. Her habit of sitting pale and naked at the breakfast table, cutting up whatever fruit they had into three portions, or sitting down with fried eggs made him once whisper to her that she was beautiful. "I'm terrific over eggs," she shot back, her mouth full. She did not get dressed. She planned to go back to bed as soon as Patrick left for the tannery and Hana left for school. Alice worked in the evenings.

His relationship with Hana was clearer. There would always be something careful about her. As if she had been badly scalded and so would approach all water tentatively for fear it was boiling. With her there would be brief conflicts, a discussion, and then everything was settled. She would not be bossed and she was self-sufficient. She didn't expect forgiveness.

They sat at the round tables at the Balkan Café eating a large meal and with ice creams strolled over at ten to the Parrot Theatre to pick up Alice. They had all the time in the world,

Hana translating the information she received on the street, speaking to a butcher who walked beside them for a hundred yards carrying a pig's head. Patrick watched the gestures towards him. They knew who he was now. A hat raised off a head in slow motion, a woman's nod to his left shoulder.

He lived – in his job and during these evening walks – in a silence, with noise and conversation all around him. To be understood, his reactions had to exaggerate themselves. The family idiot. A stroke victim. "Paderick," the shopkeepers would call him as he handed them money and a list of foods Hana had written out in Macedonian, accepting whatever they gave him. He felt himself expand into an innocent. Every true thing he learned about character he learned at this time in his life. Once, when they were at the Teck Cinema watching a Chaplin film he found himself laughing out loud, joining the others in their laughter. And he caught someone's eye, the body bending forward to look at him, who had the same realization – that this mutual laughter was conversation.

He was always comfortable in someone else's landscape, enjoyed being taught the customs of a place. Patrick wanted the city Hana had constructed for herself – the places she brought together and held as if on the delicate thread of her curiosity: Hoo's Trading Company where Alice bought herbs for fever, gaslit diners whose aquarium windows leaned against the street. They watched the water-nymph follies at Sunnyside Park, watched the Italian gymnasts at the Elm Street gym, heard the chanting of English lessons to large groups at Central Neighbourhood House – one pure English voice claiming *My name is Ernest*, and then a barrage of male voices claiming their names were Ernest.

But Hana's favourite place of spells was the Geranium Bakery, and one Saturday afternoon she took him there to meet her friend Nicholas. She guided Patrick among the other workers and sacks of flour and rollers towards Nicholas Temelcoff, who turned towards her and stretched his arms out wide. It was a joke, he was covered in flour and did not really expect to be embraced. He shook Patrick's hand and began to show them around the bakery, Hana scooping bits of raw dough with her finger and eating them. Temelcoff was meticulously dressed in jacket and tie but wore no apron so that the flour dust continued to settle on him as he moved through the bakery. He pulled chains that hung from the ceiling to start rollers moving on the upper level. He brought a small doll out of his pocket and handed it to Hana – and this time she embraced him, her head on his chest. The two men had said no more than four polite sentences to each other by the time Patrick left with the girl.

One night Hana pulled out a valise from under the bed and showed him some mementoes. There was a photograph of her as a baby – with her first nickname, Piko, scrawled in pencil on it. Three other photographs: a group of men working on the Bloor Street Viaduct, a photograph of Alice in a play at the Finnish Labour Temple, three men standing in snow in a lumber camp. A sumac bracelet. A rosary. These objects spread out on the bed replaced her father's absence.

So he discovered Cato through the daughter. The girl had been told everything about him, told of his charm, his cruelty, his selfishness, his heroism, the way he had met and seduced Alice. "You didn't know Cato, did you?" "No." "Well he was supposed to be very passionate, very cruel." "Don't talk like that, Hana, you're ten years old, and he's your father." "Oh, I love him, even if I never met him. That's just the truth."

She was totally unlike Patrick, always practical. When he returned from the steambaths on the first Saturday she had inquired about the price and he saw her trying to work out if it was worth it. "I would have paid anything," he muttered, and he saw she could not understand or accept such extravagance in him. She thought him foolish. In the same way, her portrait of her father lacked any sentimentality.

– Who were those people in the bridge picture, Hana?
– Oh she must have known them.

*　　*　　*

Alice was in sunlight on the grass slope leading down from the waterworks, looking out onto the lake, her hand keeping the sun out of her eyes. "I had to learn I couldn't trust him. Not that he ever wanted me to. You must realize that Cato was not his real name, it was his war name. And who knows who he was with or what he was doing on a Wednesday or a Friday. He was self-made. He worked hard, he spoke out. On Thursdays he came shimmering along on his bike, dropped his tackle in the hall as if he were a hurried fisherman, and said, *Let's go!*"

– How long did you stay together?
– Till he died. We were always breaking up. He thought his life was too complicated. We spent half our time worrying with each other about this. And then on Wednesday nights I would dream out the next afternoon on our bicycles along that stretch of road, in April flood or summer dust. You could blindfold me now, Patrick, and I would be able to take you there, fifty yards off the road, across a creek – lots of mud here, turn right – this is where we always got our feet wet, some gum off a low

140

pine on my hair as I'd leap the creek. Shoulder-high cattails and ferns, then into the longhouse of cedars. Spring crows in the cedar branches! Needles on the earth half a foot deep! When we made love there he would bury something, a small bottle, a pencil, a handkerchief, a sock. He left something everywhere we made love. Such sexual archaeology. There was a piece of wood that looked like the roof of a doghouse. When we got lost we'd always have to look for that – when snow changed the shape of trees or fall made skeletons of everything, or in summer when everything was overgrown chaos. We would go there all through the year, every season, and winter was strangely easier than summer with its bugs and deer flies. We could make hollows in the snow, we were protected from wind by the trees. It is important to be close to the surface of the earth.

He began to like it, I think, us not being lovers indoors. Still, we always fought. I told him once if he ever broke up with me and said we were 'crazy' and that we had to stop, I would knife him.

– You told me that too.

– I feel charmed, Patrick, that I knew him as well as I know you.

– I feel jealous. No. I don't feel jealous.

– Because he's dead? You listen to me so calmly, all this intimacy. . . .

– Hana showed me the pictures. Who were the men on the bridge?

– That's the past, Patrick, leave it alone. Anyway, you should get Hana to talk to you about Cato and the socks. That's her favourite story.

"They were in the woods and came into a field to get away from the bugs. It was summer. Lots of bugs, my mom said. So they took off their clothes and went for a swim in the river. When they came back, there were all these young bulls where their clothes were. About five of them in a circle around the clothes. Only they were not interested in the clothes except for his socks! They were sniffing them up in the air and tossing them back and forth. It really embarrassed Cato. My mom told me he didn't want to talk about it to others. I just love that – all those serious bulls throwing his socks back and forth. Mom thinks they were very excited."

Patrick had the photograph from Hana's suitcase in his pocket. In books he had read, even those romances he swallowed during childhood, Patrick never believed that characters lived only on the page. They altered when the author's eye was somewhere else. Outside the plot there was a great darkness, but there would of course be daylight elsewhere on earth. Each character had his own time zone, his own lamp, otherwise they were just men from nowhere.

He was in the Riverdale Library looking for any reference to the building of the Bloor Street Viaduct. He collected the newspapers and journals he needed and went and sat in the Boys and Girls Room with its high rafters and leaded windows that let in oceans of light. He revelled in this room, the tiny desks, the smell of books. It was how he imagined the dining hall of a submarine would look.

He read the descriptions of the bridge's opening on October 18, 1918. One newspaper had a picture of a cyclist racing across. He worked backwards. It had taken only two years to build. It had taken years before that to agree on how it was to be done, Commissioner Harris' determination forcing it through. He looked at the various photographs: the shells of wood structures into which concrete was poured, and then the wood removed like hardened bandages to reveal the piers. He read up on everything – survey arguments, the scandals, the deaths of workers fleetingly mentioned, the story of the young nun who had fallen off the bridge, the body never found. He read about the flooding Don River underneath, ice dangers, the decision to use night crews and the night deaths that followed. There was an article on daredevils. He heard the library bell. He turned the page to the photograph of them and he pulled out the picture he had and laid it next to the one in the newspaper. Third from the left, the newspaper said, was Nicholas Temelcoff.

Leaving the library, Patrick crossed Broadview Avenue and began walking east. He paused, suddenly stilled, wanting to go back, but the library was closed now and it would be pointless. They would not print the photograph of a nun. A dead or a missing nun.

He took a step forward. Now he was walking slowly, approaching a street-band, and the click of his footsteps unconsciously adapted themselves to the music that began to surround him. The cornet and saxophone and drum chased each other across solos and then suddenly, as Patrick drew alongside them, fell together and rose within a chorus.

He saw himself gazing at so many stories — knowing of Alice's lover Cato and Hana's wanderings in the baker's world. He walked on beyond the sound of the street musicians, aware once again of the silence between his individual steps, knowing now he could add music by simply providing the thread of a hum. He saw the interactions, saw how each one of them was carried by the strength of something more than themselves.

If Alice had been a nun . . .

The street-band had depicted perfect company, with an ending full of embraces after the solos had made everyone stronger, more delineated. His own life was no longer a single story but part of a mural, which was a falling together of accomplices. Patrick saw a wondrous night web – all of these fragments of a human order, something ungoverned by the family he was born into or the headlines of the day. A nun on a bridge, a dare-devil who was unable to sleep without drink, a boy watching a fire from his bed at night, an actress who ran away with a mil-lionaire – the detritus and chaos of the age was realigned.

*　　*　　*

The articles and illustrations he found in the Riverdale Library depicted every detail about the soil, the wood, the weight of concrete, everything but information on those who actually built the bridge. There were no photographers like Lewis Hine, who in the United States was photographing child labour every-where – trapper boys in coal mines, seven-year-old doffer girls in New England mills. *To locate the evils and find the hidden purity.* Official histories and news stories were always soft as rhetoric, like that of a politician making a speech after a bridge is built, a man who does not even cut the grass on his own lawn. Hine's photographs betray official history and put together another family. The man with the pneumatic drill on the Empire State Building in the fog of stone dust, a tenement couple, breaker boys in the mines. His photographs are rooms one can step into – cavernous buildings where a man turns a wrench the size of his body, or caves of iron where the white faces give the young children working there the terrible look of ghosts. But Patrick would never see the great photographs of Hine, as he would never read the letters of Joseph Conrad.

Official histories, news stories surround us daily, but the events of art reach us too late, travel languorously like messages in a bottle.

Only the best art can order the chaotic tumble of events. Only the best can realign chaos to suggest both the chaos and order it will become.

Within two years of 1066, work began on the Bayeux Tapestry, Constantin the African brought Greek medicine to the western world. The chaos and tumble of events. The first sentence of every novel should be: "Trust me, this will take time but there is order here, very faint, very human." Meander if you want to get to town.

*   *   *

I have taught you that the sky in all its zones is mortal.

Her favourite sentence hovers next to Patrick as he wakens. By dawn he is on the livid floor of the tannery with the curved pilot knife. All day long as he cuts into the leather his mind moves over the few details she has given him about her life. Even in the farmhouse at Paris Plains there had been a silence about her youth, even with Cato she gave out only his war name. If Alice Gull had been a nun? A rosary, a sumac bracelet . . .

At six in the evening he returns from work and her open palms press into his ribs. He lifts Alice into his arms and Hana jumps onto her mother's back. So they move, cumbersome, through the small room, falling onto the bed. The game is that Hana has to try and push them off, putting her feet against the wall and her shoulders against them. Then they are on the floor and Hana falls on top. Then he and Hana try to lift Alice back onto the bed.

He is always surprised at Alice's body. She seems physically frail, as if a jostle will break her, but she is agile, a dancer as much as an actress moving fluidly through rooms. She thinks the twentieth century's greatest invention is the jitterbug. She can almost forgive capitalism for that. She is in love with Fats Waller. Patrick has seen her sit at the piano in the Balkan Café and sing

> *"Needed no star*
> *Wanted no moon*
> *Always thought it too dumb . . .*
> *Then all at once*
> *Up jumped you*
> *With love."*

Clara, she would say later, was the classical one, *she* could play the piano like a queen stepping across mud. I play the way I think. And heartbreaking romance is all I want in music.

But Alice's tenderest speech to him, as she sat on his belly looking down, concerned her missing of Clara. "I love Clara," she said to him, the lover of Clara. "I miss her. She made me sane for all those years. That was important for what I am now."

She could move like . . . she could sing as low as. . . . Why is it that I am now trying to uncover every facet of Alice's nature for myself?

He wants everything of Alice to be with him here in this

room as if she is not dead. As if he can be given that gift, to relive those days when Alice was with him and Hana, which in literature is the real gift. He turns the page backwards. Once more there is the image of them struggling and tickling Alice until she releases her grip on her shirt and it comes off with a flourish, and Hana jumps up, waving it like a rebel's flag in the small green-painted room. All these fragments of memory . . . so we can retreat from the grand story and stumble accidentally upon a luxury, one of those underground pools where we can sit still. Those moments, those few pages in a book we go back and forth over.

*   *   *

Nicholas Temelcoff's fingers sink into a ball of dough and pull it apart, then they reassemble it and fling it down onto the table. He looks up and sees Patrick enter the Geranium Bakery, awkwardly look around, and then approach him. Patrick pulls out the photograph and places it in front of Temelcoff.

Behind them the pulleys and rollers move hundreds of loaves into the ovens, pause, then continue out. Temelcoff in his grey clothes talks with Patrick about the bridge and the nun – reminded of the exact date which his memory had lost – and pleasure and wonder fill him. He stands in the centre of the bakery thinking, throwing a small ball of dough up and catching it, unaware of this gesture for so long that Patrick, a yard from him, cannot reach him. Temelcoff is somewhere else, the eyes magnified behind the spectacles, the ball of dough falling surely back into the hand, the arm that caught her in the air and pulled her back into life. "*Talk, you must talk,*" and so mockingly she took a parrot's name. *Alicia.*

Nicholas Temelcoff never looks back. He will drive the bakery van over the bridge with his wife and children and only casually mention his work there. He is a citizen here, in the present, successful with his own bakery. His bread and rolls and cakes and pastries reach the multitudes in the city. He is a man who is comfortable among ovens, the smell of things rising, the metamorphosis of food. But he pauses now, reminded about the details of the incident on the bridge.

He stands exactly where Patrick left him, thinking, as those would who believe that to continue a good dream you must lie down the next night in exactly the same position you awakened in, where the body parted from its images. Nicholas is aware of himself standing there within the pleasure of recall. It is something new to him. This is what history means. He came to this country like a torch on fire and he swallowed air as he walked forward and he gave out light. Energy poured through him. That was all he had time for in those years. Language, customs, family, salaries. Patrick's gift, that arrow into the past, shows him the wealth in himself, how he has been sewn into history. Now he will begin to tell stories. He is a tentative man, even with his family. That night in bed shyly he tells his wife the story of the nun.

Cato would always arrive late, Alice remembers, his bicycle clanging to the pavement outside her window. She would climb onto the handlebars and they'd weave down to the lake laid out like crinoline. They'd lie against the railway embankment a few yards from Lake Ontario. The branches in winter were encased in ice and she would lean her head back, exposing her white neck, and take twig and icicle in her mouth and snap it off with the pressure of her tongue.

But at other times she was glad she didn't live with him permanently, to be pulled continually by his planet. If you were close to Cato you had to be a representative of his world, his friends, his plans for the week. Strangers, old lovers, ambled up to him on the street and embraced him and *they* had to join the group. It was impossible to go two blocks on a bicycle with him without running into someone who needed help to find a friend or move a cabinet. "Just *one day*, Cato," she'd say. "Even *four hours*!"

And so he became the man who was Thursday to her. They disappeared into the ravines, the woods north of the city, or her favourite place – against the thick stones of the railway embankment, the willow bending over clothed in ice, loving each other along with the sound of the spring breakup. Kissing each other with stones in their mouths. The freeze still over the March lake, she would lie on her stomach, his hand under her,

150

the shudder of the passing train, the Apalachicola boxcars, reaching through his palm to her breast.

So Thursday jumped out of the week like a fold-out bed. But there were no beds for them ever. By the time Hana was born he was dead.

Patrick laid his head on her stomach, watching the secret lift of her skin at each heartbeat. Talking on the nights they could afford to stay up late. "He was born up north, you know, quite near where he died." Her hand brushed against his chest. "His father moved here from Finland as a logger. Here his family no longer had to bow to priests or dignitaries and they were soon involved in the unions. Cato was born here. His father skated three miles for the doctor the night he was born. He skated across the lake holding up cattails on fire."

Patrick stopped her hand moving.

— So they were *Finns*.
— What?
— Finns. When I was a kid . . .

Now in his thirties he finally had a name for that group of men he witnessed as a child.

She looked at Patrick, who was smiling as if a riddle old and tiresome had been solved, a burr plucked from his brain. In the green room the moon showed her face clearly. A moon returning from when he was eleven. He loved the power of coincidence, the pleasure of strangeness. *Hello Finland!*

— Come into me.

And who was she? And where was she from? His hands on her shoulders, his arms straight, so their upper torsos were separate, their faces apart. The brain and eyes interpreting pleasure in the other, these textures that brushed and gripped. He pivoted on her hands against his belly, moving deeper, moving back, and was still. Not a movement of the eye. He knew now he was the sum of all he had been in his life since he was that boy in the snow woods, her hands collapsing to hold him against her harder. Fingernail at his spine. His cheek against her turquoise eye.

He lay in bed looking at the light of the moon in the bones of the fire escape. The light of the electric clock advertising Cabinet Cigars. Out there the beautiful grey of the Victory Flour Mills at midnight, its clean curves over the lake. Any decade you wished.

– God I love your face . . .

She has delivered him out of nothing. This woman who jumps onto him laughing in mid-air and growls at his neck and pulls him like a wheel over her.

How can she who had torn his heart open at the waterworks with her art lie now like a human in his arms? Or stand catatonic in front of bananas on Eastern Avenue deciding which bunch to buy. Does this make her more magical? As if a fabulous heron in flight has fallen dead at his feet and he sees the further wonder of its meticulous construction. How did someone conceive of putting this structure of bones and feathers together, deciding on the weight of beak and skull, and give it the ability to fly?

His love of the theatre was that of an amateur. He picked up gossip, mementoes, handbills. He loved technique, to walk backstage and see Ophelia with her mad face half rubbed off. This was humanity in theatre, the scar – the old actor famous for playing whimsical judges, who rode the Queen streetcar east of the city and ate his dinner alone before joining his sleeping wife. Patrick liked that. He wanted to be fooled by the person he felt could not fool him, who stopped three yards past the side curtain and became somebody else.

But with Alice, after the episode at the waterworks and in other performances, he can never conceive how she leaps from her true self to her other true self. It is a flight he knows nothing about. He cannot put the two people together. Did the actor – holding her on stage, reciting wondrous language, holding his painted face inches away from her painted face, kissing her ear in drawing-room comedies – know the person she had stepped from to be there?

In the midst of his love for Alice, in the midst of lovemaking even, he watches her face waiting for her to be translated into this war bride or that queen or shopgirl, half expecting metamorphosis as they kiss. Annunciation. The eye would go first, and as he draws back he will be in another country, another century, his arms around a stranger.

There had been an earring missing beside the bed or at the sink in the kitchen. He had watched her move around the room half-naked, dressing, bending down to a pile of clothes in his room without furniture, a long time ago, saying *Can't find my earring, does it matter?* As if another woman would find it. Alice departing with one ear undressed. *If we meet again we can say hello, we can say goodbye.*

Dear Alice —

*The only heat in this bunkhouse is from a small
drum stove. In the evenings air is thick from the damp
clothes in the rafters above the fire and from tobacco
smoke. To avoid suffocating, the men in the upper
bunks push out the moss chinking between logs.*

Patrick reads slowly, knowing he will be given the letter only
once, on this summer night under the one lightbulb of the
room, far from winter weather. Hana sits on the bed and
watches him. For what? He thinks as he reads what his face
should express to the letter-writer's daughter. He holds the
grade-school notebook which the words fill. She has removed it
from the suitcase and presented it to him. *Dear Alice,* scrawled,
the handwriting large and hurried but the information detailed
as if Cato were trying to hold everything he saw, at the lumber
camp near Onion Lake, during his final days.

*I write at a table hammered permanently into the
floor. The log bunks are nailed into the walls. Fires die
out at night and men wake with hair frozen to damp
icicles on the wall. "In the bleak mid-winter — Frosty
wind made moan — Earth stood hard as iron — Water
like a stone." That was the first hymn I learned in*

154

English, written by someone in an English village.
And it describes this place better than anything else.

Patrick sees Cato writing by tallow light . . . sealing the letter, passing the package to someone leaving the camp the next morning. When Alice opens the package five weeks later she pulls the exercise book to her face and smells whatever she can of him, for he has been dead a month. She smells the candle-wax, she imagines the odour of the hut, the cold pencil he has sharpened before beginning to write his unsigned letters about camp conditions and strike conditions. Cato sits dead centre, at the food table, the pipe smoke moves live and grey around him. His hair smells of it, it has entered deep into his shirt and sweater, it hangs against his stubbled beard.

None of the camp bosses knows who he is or of his connection to the planned strike. But they soon discover this. He slips out of the lumber camp on foot and goes into open snow country. The nearest town is Port Arthur, over a hundred and twenty miles away, and he aims himself towards it.

Four men on horseback attempt to capture Cato over the next week. But Cato knows snow country; he was born into it. He can, it seems, disappear under the surface of it. He avoids the familiar route, sleeps in trees, even risks crawling on all fours over thin-iced lakes – hearing the surface crack and groan under him. Now and then he sees flares belonging to his hunters. At each camp he writes into a notebook, jams it into a tin, and buries the tin deep under the snow or ties it onto a high branch. Meanwhile his package of letters is travelling, passed from hand to hand before it nestles in a bag next to a rolled-up swede saw on a logger's back on the final leg of the journey.

While he is cutting a hole in the ice at Onion Lake, Cato sees the men. They ride out of the trees and execute him. They find no messages or identification on him. They try burning the body but he will not ignite. There have been union men before him and there will be union men after him. The man with the swede saw posts his bundle of letters in Algoma unaware that the sender is dead, shot to death, buried in the ice of a shallow river.

> They lose two days a month because of wet weather.
> Travelling eats up $10 a season; mitts $6; shoes and
> stockings $25; working clothes $35. Being forced to
> buy their supplies in camps means 30 per cent tagged
> onto city prices . . .

Patrick reads, aware that the smell of smoke is no longer on the porous paper. The words on the page form a rune – flint-hard and unemotional in the midst of the inferno of Cato's situation.

And who is he to touch the lover of this man, to eat meals with his daughter, to stand dazed under a lightbulb and read his last letter?

He remains standing alone in the room Hana has now left. She had seen him hypnotized, as if the letter stared back at him. He realizes what he is doing, that he has become a searcher again with this family. As if he had leaned forward to the woman he had just met in Paris Plains and said, Who is your lover? Tell me the most painful thing that has happened to you. For he has over the years learned the answers. He holds now the last ten minutes of Cato's language. In his mind he sees Alice pick up the package which death has made impossible – after the murder, the discovery of the body in ice, his burial, and the acquittal of the bosses at the inquiry.

Patrick has clung like moss to strangers, to the nooks and fissures of their situations. He has always been alien, the third person in the picture. He is the one born in this country who knows nothing of the place. The Finns of his childhood used the river, even knew it by night, the men of burning rushes delirious in the darkness. This he had never done. He was a watcher, a corrector. He could no more have skated along the darkness of a river than been the hero of one of these stories. Alice had once described a play to him in which several actresses shared the role of the heroine. After half an hour the powerful matriarch removed her large coat from which animal pelts dangled and she passed it, along with her strength, to one of the minor characters. In this way even a silent daughter could put on the cloak and be able to break through her chrysalis into language. Each person had their moment when they assumed the skins of wild animals, when they took responsibility for the story.

Clara and Ambrose and Alice and Temelcoff and Cato – this cluster made up a drama without him. And he himself was nothing but a prism that refracted their lives. He searched out things, he collected things. He was an abashed man, an inheritance from his father. Born in Abashed, Ontario. What did the word mean? Something that suggested there was a terrible horizon in him beyond which he couldn't leap. Something hollow, so when alone, when not aligned with another – whether it was Ambrose or Clara or Alice – he could hear the rattle within that suggested a space between him and community. A gap of love.

He had lived in this country all of his life. But it was only now that he learned of the union battles up north where Cato was murdered some time in the winter of 1921, and found under the ice of a shallow creek near Onion Lake a week after he had written his last letter. The facts of the story had surrounded Hana since birth, it was a part of her. And all of his life Patrick had been oblivious to it, a searcher gazing into the darkness of his own country, a blind man dressing the heroine.

Every Sunday they still congregated at the waterworks. They walked over grills under which foam rushed, they opened doorways to waterfalls. The building, now three-quarters finished, spread ceremonial over the rise just south of Queen Street, looking onto the lake. Because of its structure the main pumping station could be filled with lamps and no light would be betrayed to the outside world. The sound of pumps churning drowned out the noise of their meetings.

On Sundays, as darkness fell, the various groups walked up to the building from the lakeshore where they would not be seen. There was food, entertainment, political speeches. A man who mimicked the King of England stepped forward with a monologue summarizing the news of the past week. Numerous communities and nationalities spoke and performed in their own languages. When they finished, the halls were cleaned up, the floors swept.

Patrick and Alice walked home along Queen Street. The girl was asleep in Patrick's arms, so at some point, tired from her weight, they would sit on a bench and lay Hana out, her head on Alice's lap. He loved this part of the city, the evening streets an extension of his limbs.

> – I want to look after Hana.
> – You already do.
> – More formally. If that will help.

– She knows you love her.

A July night. On what summer night was it that she spoke of Clara and how she missed her? All these incidents and emotions to cover and the story like a tired child tugging us on, not letting us converse with ease, sleeping on our shoulder so it is difficult to embrace the person we love. He loved Alice. He leaned against her and he could feel her hair still wet from the sweat of the performance.

– You will catch a cold.
– Ah yes.

* * *

Now he aches for her smallness, her intricacy – he needs a second glance whenever he thinks of her. In the middle of a field she removes her blouse. Sightings of her breasts. *Trompe l'oeil.* An artist has picked up a pencil and made a fine crosshatched shadow and so they come into existence. He sits and watches her sniffing the wind across a field. The woman he looked through when in love with Clara. Clara's eclipse. The phrase like a flower or event named during the last century.

During Cato's funeral, while Alice held the infant Hana, there was an eclipse. The mourners stood still while the Finnish Brass Band played Chopin's "Funeral March" into the oncoming darkness and throughout the seventeen minutes of total eclipse. The music a lifeline from one moment of light to another.

Now he aches for her, for those days that belonged to the moon. They would sit side by side in a Chinese restaurant, empty but for the two of them. Wanting to face each other but wanting to hold each other and having to decide on one pleasure. The intricate choices of desire.

I don't think I'm big enough to put someone in a position where they will hurt another. That's what you said, Alice, that made me love you most. Made me trust you. No one else would have worried about that, could have said it and made me believe it, that first night in your room. Every bird and insect froze into the element of air at that moment when the sentence slid up, palpable, out of your mouth. You unaware you were expressing a tenderness, thinking you were being critical of yourself.

And another gesture of yours at a dance. I was dancing with someone else and could see you, dying to dance, and stepping up to a man and delicately tapping him on his shoulder, a shy yet determined expression on your face.

They sit in a field. They sit in the red and yellow and gold decor of the restaurant, empty in the late afternoon but for them. Hunger and desire spiriting him across the city, onto trolley after trolley, in order to reach her arm, her neck, this Chinese restaurant, that Macedonian café, this field he is now in the centre of with her. There are country houses on the periphery so they have walked to its centre, the distant point, to be alone.

He will turn while walking and see the fragility of her breasts – the result of a pencil's shading.

She drops into his arms, held out stern as a school desk. He walks then, he dances with the wheat in his hands. When he was twelve he turned the pages always towards illustration and saw the heroes carry the women across British Columbian streams, across the foot of waterfalls. And now her hand above her eyes shielding out the sun. Her shirt on her lap. He has come across a love story. This is only a love story. He does not wish for plot and all its consequences. Let me stay in this field with Alice Gull....

REMORSE

H E HAD ALWAYS wanted to know her when she was old.
Patrick sits in her green room, in front of leaves and ber-
ries in the old river bottle – a bouquet of weeds collected by
Alice the day before her death. Sumac and valley grasses that
she picked under the viaduct. When night comes he lights the
kerosene lamp, which throws a shadow of this still-life against
the wall so it flickers dark and alive.

Let me now re-emphasize the extreme looseness of the struc-
ture of things. Whispered to him once.

He undresses and climbs into the bed, where there is the
smell of her, where he is unable to sleep. He stays in her room,
he escorts her last flowers through death and afterlife, after
whatever spirit in them has evaporated out of their brownness.
He knows he doesn't have long before he loses the exact memory of her face. His mind moves closer to the skin at the side of
her nose where the scar lies. She was always too conscious of it,
a line she assumed unbalanced her face. How can he evoke her
without this fine line?

He had wanted to know her when she was old. At lunches she
would argue her ideas against him, holding up her glass, "To
impatience! To the evolving human!" while he was intent on
her shoulder, romantic towards the dazzle of her hair. Her grin
was always there when he spoke of growing old with her – as if

163

she had made some other pact, as if there was another arrow of alliance. He couldn't wait to know her when, in years to come, they would be solvent, sexually calmer, less like wildlife. There was always, he thought, this pleasure ahead of him, an ace of joy up his sleeve so he could say you can do anything to me, take everything away, put me in prison, but I will know Alice Gull when we are old. Even if we cannot be lovers I will come each afternoon, come as if courting, and over lunch we will share our thoughts, laughing, so this talk will be love.

He had wanted that. And what had she wanted?

> – I was happiest when I was pregnant. When I *bloomed*.
> – I don't understand why you like me.
> – I feel good about myself since I met you. Since the days with Clara, when you could see nothing else but her and I was watching you. I wasn't jealous. I wasn't in love with you. I was learning wonderful things then, with Clara. You and I will never enter certain rooms together, Patrick. A woman needs a woman to laugh with, over some things. Clara and I felt like a planet! But there was a time after that when I went under. And you gave me an energy. A confidence.

Now there is a moat around her he will never cross again. He will not even cup his hands to drink its waters. As if, having travelled all that distance to enter the castle in order to learn its wisdom for the grand cause, he now turns and walks away.

*   *   *

Patrick steps out of the Verral Avenue rooms. He enters Union Station and, once he is travelling, the landscape slurs into darkness. He focuses thirty yards past the train window until his mind locks, thinking of nothing, not even the death of Alice. By his feet is a black cardboard suitcase. He can think now only of objects. Something alive, just one small grey bird on a branch, will break his heart.

The night train travelling north to Huntsville contains a regatta crowd – men in straw boaters and silk scarves jubilant around him. They weave towards the sleeping cars, passing Patrick, who stands in the corridor, their drunk bodies brushing against him. He gazes through his reflection, hypnotized by the manic parade of sky and rock and tree and moon. No resolution or pause. *Alice*. . . . He breathes out a dead name. Only a dead name is permanent.

Rectangles of light sweep along the earth. He walks to the end of the corridor, opens the door, and stands in the no man's land between carriages, holding onto the stiff accordion-like walls, within the violent rattle of the train.

Alice had an idea, a cause in her eye about wealth and power, forever and ever. And at the end as she turned round to him on the street hearing her name yelled, surprised at Patrick being near, there was nothing completed or attained. And he could think of nothing but the eyes looking for him above the terrible wound suddenly appearing as she turned.

They arrive in Huntsville at three in the morning. Patrick watches a porter travel the corridor of sleeping berths, tagging the shoes left out to be cleaned, and return a few minutes later with a sack into which he throws them all. The passengers will not be awakened until seven.

The stewards sit on the steps of the train polishing shoes.

They speak quietly, smoking cigarettes. Patrick sees them in the yellow spray of the station lamp. He strolls to the end of the platform where there is darkness. Bush. He feels transparent, minuscule. Civilization now, on this August night, is two men cleaning shoes as they sit on the steps of a train. He looks at them from the darkness. He has walked through the pools of light hanging over this platform and light has not attached itself to him. Walking through rain would have left him wet. But light, or a man polishing one tan shoe at four A.M., is only an idea. And this will not convert Patrick, whose loss creates venom. At times like this he could put his hand under the wheel of a train to spite the driver. He could pick up a porcupine and thrash it against the fence not caring how many quills were flung into his hands and neck in retaliation.

At eight A.M. the passengers walk from the train, sleepy, dazed by their own movement, to the dock belonging to the Huntsville and Lake-of-Bays Navigation Company. Patrick carries his fragile suitcase and boards *The Algonquin* steamer.

Most of the regatta crowd will be guests at either Bigwin Inn or the Muskoka Hotel. Patrick watches the scenery as the boat passes the thick-treed islands. Now and then there is a clearing of lawn imposed on the landscape. The setting seems strangely spartan to attract so many wealthy people, to be the playground of the rich. He finds a deck-chair and sleeps, and even in sleep his hand clutches the suitcase. He wakes to every hoot of the whistle as the boat winds its way through North Portage. When they pass Bigwin Island, they are greeted by the Anglo-Canadian Band playing on the rock promontory – tubas, trumpets, violins, and various other instruments. Patrick waves along with the others. He will not be coming back this way. He might as well wave now.

In the Garden of the Blind, on Page Island, a stone cherub holds out a hand from which water leaps up into the air. A tree full of birds spreads itself high over the southern area of the lawn. There is a falling of sounds – bird-calls like drops of water – onto the blind woman sitting there. Seeds float down onto the gravel borders, a sound path for those walking without sight. On one of the benches, under the tree, Patrick sits reading the newspaper.

If he closes his eyes, these noises will overpower him, in the way he imagines the cherub accepts that water which leaps from his palm into air and then falls back onto his face. He watches a bird dart. The woman on his right hears the rustle of his news-paper and realizes he is alien here.

He is one island over from last night's fire, hiding now in this garden, unseen among the blind, till nightfall.

He had loosened the cap on the paraffin can and enclosed it gur-gling within his black cardboard suitcase. Then he began his walk along the mezzanine of the empty Muskoka Hotel. He had waited until the guests and staff were outside on the lawns, busy with the regatta dinner. He leaned over the banister to look at the stuffed animal-heads below him, the liquid leaking down, then walked on, the suitcase innocent in his right hand, down the stairs to the lobby. The smell was evident now. *Fire!*

he yelled. He lit a match, dropped it, and the fire ran upstairs and round and round the circular mezzanine. His arm was on fire. He plunged the sleeve of his jacket into an aquarium. The suitcase at the foot of the stairs exploded. He moved alone through the lobby of the Muskoka Hotel, the deerheads above him on fire.

He walked from the fire towards the water. As he made his way to the rowboat, he checked the explosive hidden under the dock. Everyone on the blue evening lawn looked at the flames, dumbfounded. Some men saw him unhook the boat and pointed. Patrick stood in the boat and waved. They waved back uncertainly, then started to run towards the dock casually, in case Patrick turned out to be a friend, then jumped onto the dock and began running towards him.

He lit the fuse, which raced towards the two men and started to row away from the dock. The fuse, like a nervy kid, buzzed and ran under the men's feet. They stopped and turned. Now they realized what it was. The older man leaped into the water and the other, his hands on his hips, paused as the blue fizzing ran into the small explosion that separated the dock from the shore.

What he begins to witness now, in the Garden of the Blind, is not sound but smell – the plants chosen with care so visitors can move from fragrance to fragrance with precise antennae. To his left he can smell mock orange. He leans over the raised bed – three feet higher than the path – and sniffs deeply.

Patrick hears footsteps and a hand touches his back. The blind woman who heard the rustle of newspapers now attaches herself to him.

– You can see, she says.

– Yes.

She smiles.

– You have a loud nose.

Her name is Elizabeth, and she offers to show him the garden. She mentions that her sister is better at identifying flowers and herbs because she does not drink. "I drink like a porpoise but only from the afternoon on. Tragic love affair in my thirties." They walk together and Patrick watches how her relaxed body drifts in this world, moving surely towards the basil and broadleaf sorrel. She lowers her hand in passing to brush the soft silk of the foliage called Rabbit's Grass. Her garden is a ballroom and she introduces him to the intimacies of dill and caraway, those shy sisters; she advises him to bend down and bruise certain leaves which are too subtle for him to appreciate when untouched.

"To focus your nasal powers you must forget about sounds. The bird sounds here are lovely but sometimes I come here drunk or with a hangover and the noise is awful. Then I want to pour medicinal fluids into my handkerchief, climb into the branches, and chloroform them." In the centre of the garden just north of the water-splashed cherub is another tree where there are no birds. "You must be looking at the camphor . . . birds recognize death better than us. Plants have complex genealogies. To a bird a succulent fruit must first be judged by its bloodlines. You may like cashew nuts or mango, or find sumac beautiful, but a bird knows that these are all, strangely, part of the poison-ivy family."

She leads him towards the imported exotics – fruitless persimmon, and the *pimpernella*, which is anise. She is curious about him but he will not say very much though he is courteous and he likes her. He will have to stay here till night and then try to swim from the island out to a boat. Along the beds on the east side of the garden there is tarragon and lavender and cardamom. She puts her hands up bluntly to his face and searches him. She finds a welt by his ear.

> – Put perumel on this. A balm.
> – I am wanted by the police.
> – For?
> – For wilful destruction of property.

She laughs.

> – Don't resent your life.

They are a frieze, a statue in this garden, a woman with her soft palms covering a tall man's face, blinding him.

When she moves her hands away from his eyes she feels the gasp on his face which is not shock or disgust but something else.

> – What is it?

Her green eye echoes somewhere within him. *Aetias Luna* – and its Canadian name, *papillon lune*. Lunar moth. Moon moth. Her other eye is simply not there, the old loose flesh of the eyelid covering nothing. But this eye is forest green, moth green, darting all over as if to catch his gaze, moving with delight over his shoulders, alighting on his ear, his nose. He had loved the lunar moth, its flare of the lower wing like a signature, a papyrus textured object whose small furred body he used to see pulsing on a branch or rock within his lantern light. The woman shifts the watery green mirror of her eye attempting to reflect everything around her.

– What is it?

Patrick allows her to guide him back to the bench. They sit and she grips his hand, not letting go of him. He feels she receives all of his qualities, in this still garden, raucous with noise. The blue veins are narrow and clear in the tight skin of her hands. He is unable to talk, even if all he said would be hidden within her blindness. Alice Gull, he could say, who once pushed her hands up against the slope of a ceiling and spoke of a grand cause, who leapt like a live puppet into his arms, who died later on a bloody pavement, ruined in his arms.

No one else enters the garden as they sit there. Beside the wooden seat is mint pepper, rosemary. In the flower-bed to the right of where they sit is *artemesia advacumculas*, whose human name she says she doesn't know. The muscles in her hand finally loosen and he turns to look at her face. She is now resting, leaning back, gently asleep. He moves his hand from her grip and leaves her.

Now he is part of the evening water, the reflection of dock lights rolling off him. Six stars and a moon. The news of the fire has left the Muskokas in an uproar and Patrick struggles to get free of the current off Page Island in order to swim towards that boat. It has crept across the blackness of the lake at a snail's pace and is now about 500 yards off shore. A night cruise with dancing – he can hear music as he swims, voices and tambourine falling like muffled glass into the water. A half-moon, a few stars, a loop of dock lights.

Somewhere in his past he has dreamed such a moment: a criminal swimming in darkness to a lighted ship. He feels removed from any context of the world, wanting to sleep at this moment, wanting to swim back into the current he has just escaped, return to the Garden of the Blind, and sleep. But he is magnetized to the nameless steamer.

A deadhead touches him in the ribs, comes up under him, and Patrick hears himself shout out in the shriek of an animal. The dreams he had of swimming to a ship involved tropic winds and crocodiles. He splashes out to discover what touched him, but it is gone. "It was a deadhead," he says to himself, talking out loud now, determined, the fear suddenly an energy in him. Brushed by this deadhead he is fully alive, feral, exhilarated. He remembers his departure from the world, stepping out onto the *porte-cochère* of the Muskoka Hotel, flames behind him. Now he will be a member of the night. He sees his visage never emerging out of shadows. Unhistorical.

He swims on, smelling traces of hickory smoke from the campfires on the island. He is delirious with hunger. Music from the boat. *"Beware of frozen ponds, peroxide blondes, stocks and bonds...."* the singer's voice over the muffle of orchestra. And what will they do as they see him climb up a rope into their company, lake weed draped over his shoulder, the blood from the log's glance on his ribs?

He is alongside the boat, in the shadow of the moon, looking up. *The Cherokee.* The panel windows from the stateroom and lounge throw out light that falls on the water. Higher up is the open deck, the dancing couples, the band. He pulls himself up on the vertical strips of rubber that protect the sides of the steamer when it docks. He smells food on deck, climbs fast, and goes headfirst through a window and lands on a table. He is in the kitchens.

A cook turns at the crash to see Patrick on his back surrounded by double-diamond glass. Patrick puts a finger to his lips, keeping it there till the man nods and moves to close the door. Patrick gets down off the table, glass all around him. On deck the pause in conversation is replaced by louder laughter, cheers for the dropped tray or whatever they thought caused the noise. The cook walks over with a broom and sweeps while Patrick stands there removing his wet clothes. There is a cut near his ribs and on his thigh. Then the cook mimes going to sleep and is gone like a ghost out of the room. Patrick walks to the switch and dims out the kitchen light.

It must be around midnight. The noise on deck is ceaseless with the orchestra weaving its way through suspicious love, tentative love. The frail music filters down into this large kitchen which he seems to own. He knows he will be caught, probably imprisoned, but for now he thrills to this brief freedom.

He squeezes out the clothes, turns on the large ovens, spreads his shirt and trousers flat, and slides them in with a baker's paddle. Then he looks for food. There are some cooked potatoes. He pulls out a slab of raw meat from the fridge and crouches behind the counter. He eats only the potato demurely. He cuts the meat into strips with a sharp knife and eats it, licking the juice that dribbles down his arm. Now and then he gets up to drink from the taps and to keep an eye on his clothes cooking at low heat in the oven.

3

CARAVAGGIO

THERE WAS A blue tin jail roof. They were painting the Kingston Penitentiary roof blue up to the sky so that after a while the three men working on it became uncertain of clear boundaries. As if they could climb up further, beyond the tin, into that ocean above the roof.

By noon, after four hours, they felt they could walk on the blue air. The prisoners Buck and Lewis and Caravaggio knew this was a trick, a humiliation of the senses. Why an intentional blue roof? They could not move without thinking twice where a surface stopped. There were times when Patrick Lewis, government paintbrush in hand, froze. Taking a seemingly innocent step he would fall through the air and die. They were fifty yards from the ground. The paint pails were joined by rope – one on each slope – so two men could move across the long roof symmetrically. They sat on the crest of the roof during their breaks eating sandwiches, not coming down all day. They leaned the heels of their hands into the wet paint as they worked. They would scratch their noses and realize they became partly invisible. If they painted long enough they would be eradicated, blue birds in a blue sky. Patrick Lewis understood this, painting a bug that would not move away alive onto the blue metal.

Demarcation, said the prisoner named Caravaggio. *That is all we need to remember.*

And that was how he escaped – a long double belt strapped

under his shoulders attaching him to the cupola so he could hang with his arms free, splayed out, while Buck and Patrick painted him, covering his hands and boots and hair with blue. They daubed his clothes and then, laying a strip of handkerchief over his eyes, painted his face blue, so he was gone – to the guards who looked up and saw nothing there.

When the search had died down, and the lights-out whistle had gone off, Caravaggio still remained as he was, unable to see what he knew would be a sliver of new moon that gave off little light. A thief's moon. He could hear Lake Ontario in this new silence after the wind died. The flutter of sailboats. A clatter of owl claw on the tin roof. He began to move in his cocoon of dry paint – at first unable to break free of the stiffness which encased him, feeling his clothes crack as he bent his arm to remove the handkerchief. He saw nothing but the night. He unhooked the belt. Uncoiling the rope hidden around the cupola, he let himself down off the roof.

He ran through the township of Bath with the white rectangle over his eyes, looking for a hardware store he could break into. He was an exotic creature who had to escape from his blue skin before daylight. But there was not one hardware or paint shop. He broke into a clothing store and in the darkness stripped and dressed in whatever would fit him from the racks. In the rooms above the store he could hear jazz on the radio, the music a compass for him. His hands felt a mirror but he would not turn on the light. He took gloves. He jumped onto a slow milk-train and climbed onto the roof. It was raining. He removed his belt, tied himself on safely, and slept.

In Trenton he untied himself and rolled off down the embankment just as the train began to move again. He was still blue, unable to see what he looked like. He undressed and laid his clothes out on the grass so he could see them in the daylight in a human shape. He knew nothing about the town of Trenton except that it was three hours from Toronto by train. He slept again. In the late afternoon, walking in the woods that skirted the industrial section, he saw REDICK'S SASH AND DOOR FACTORY. He groomed himself as well as he could and stepped out of the trees – a green sweater, black trousers, blue boots, and a blue head.

There was a kid sitting on a pile of lumber behind the store who saw him the moment he stepped into the clearing. The boy didn't move at all, just regarded him as he walked, trying to look casual, the long twenty-five yards to the store. Caravaggio crouched in front of the boy.

> – What's your name?
> – Alfred.
> – Will you go in there, Al, and see if you can find me some turpentine?
> – Are you from the movie company?
> – The movie? He nodded.

The kid ran off and returned a few minutes later, still alone. That was good.

> – Your dad own this place?
> – No, I just like it here. All the doors propped outside, where they don't belong – things where they shouldn't be.

While the boy spoke Caravaggio tore off the tail of his shirt.

> – There is another place in town where you can see outboard motors and car engines hanging off branches.
> – Yeah? Al, can you help me get this off my face and hair?

– Sure.

They sat in the late afternoon sunlight by the doors, the boy dipping the shirt-tail into the tin and wiping the colour off Caravaggio's face. The two of them talked quietly about the other place where the engines hung from the trees. When Caravaggio unbuttoned his shirt the boy saw the terrible scars across his neck and gasped. It looked to him as if some giant bird had left claw marks from trying to lift off the man's head. Caravaggio told him to forget the movie, he was not an actor, he was from prison. "I'm Caravaggio – the painter," he laughed. The boy promised never to say anything.

They decided that his hair should be cut off, so the boy went back into the store and came back giggling and shrugging with some rose shears. Soon Caravaggio looked almost bald, certainly unrecognizable. When the owner of Redick's Door Factory was busy, Caravaggio used the bathroom, soaping and washing the turpentine off his face. He saw his neck for the first time in a mirror, scarred from the prison attack three months earlier.

In the yard the boy wrote out his name on a piece of paper. From his pocket he took out an old maple-syrup spile with the year 1882 on it, and he wrapped the paper around it. When the man came back, cleaned up, the boy handed it to him. The man said, "I don't have anything to give you now." The kid grinned, very happy. "I know," he said. "Remember my name."

He was running, his boots disappearing into grey bush. Away from Lake Ontario, travelling north where he knew he could find some unopened cottage to stay quietly for a few days. Landscape for Caravaggio was never calm. A tree bending with difficulty, a flower thrashed by wind, a cloud turning black, a cone falling – everything moved anguished at separate speeds. When he ran he saw it all. The eye splintering into fifteen sentries, watching every approach.

He ran with the Trent canal system on his right, passing the red lock buildings and their concrete platforms over the water. Every few miles he would stop and watch the glassy waters turn chaotic on the other side of the sluice gate, then he was off again. In two days he was as far north as Bobcaygeon. He slept that night among the lumber at the Boyd Sawmill and one evening later he was racing down a road. It was dusk. He had slept out three nights now. The last of the blue paint at his wrist.

The first cottages showed too many signs of life, the canoes already hauled out. He retreated back up their driveways. He came to a cottage with a glassed-in porch and green shutters, painted gables, and a double-pitch roof. If the owners arrived he could swing out of the second-floor window and walk along the roof. Caravaggio looked at architecture with a perception common to thieves who saw cupboards as having weak backs, who knew fences were easier to go through than over.

He stood breathing heavily in the dusk, looking up at the cottage, tired of running, having eaten only bits of chocolate the boy had given him. *Al.* Behind him the landscape was darkening down fast. He was inside the cottage in ten seconds.

He walked around the rooms, excited, his hand trailing off the sofa top, noticed the magazines stacked on the shelf. He turned left into a kitchen and used a knife to saw open a can. Darkness. He wanted no lights on tonight. He dug the knife into the can and gulped down beans, too hungry and tired for a spoon. Then he went upstairs and ripped two blankets off a bed and spread them out in the upstairs hall beside the window which led to the roof.

He hated the hours of sleep. He was a man who thrived and worked in available light. At night his wife would sleep in his embrace but the room around him continued to be alive, his body porous to every noise, his stare painting out darkness. He would sleep as insecurely as a thief does, which is why they are always tired.

*   *   *

He climbs into black water. A temperature of blood. He sees and feels no horizon, no edge to the liquid he is in. The night air is forensic. An animal slips into the water.

This river is not deep, he can walk across it. His boots, laces tied to each other, are hanging around his neck. He doesn't want them wet but he goes deeper and he feels them filling, the extra weight of water in them now. The floor of the river feels secure. Mud. Sticks. A bridge a hundred yards south of him made of concrete and wood. A tug at his boot beside the collarbone.

As Caravaggio sleeps, his head thrown back, witnessing a familiar nightmare, three men enter his prison cell in silence. The men enter and Patrick in the cell opposite on the next level up watches them and all language dries up. As they raise their hands over Caravaggio, Patrick breaks into a square-dance call – *"Allemande left your corners all"* – screaming it absurdly as warning up into the stone darkness. The three men turn to the sudden noise and Caravaggio is on his feet struggling out of his nightmare.

The men twist his grey sheet into a rope and wind it around his eyes and nose. Caravaggio can just breathe, he can just hear their blows as if delayed against the side of his head. They swing him tied up in the sheet until he is caught in the arms of another. Then another blow. Patrick's voice continuing to shout out, the other cells alive now and banging too. *"Birdie fly out and the crow fly in, crow fly out and give birdie a spin."* His father's language emerging from somewhere in his past, now a soundtrack for murder.

The animal from the nightmare bares its teeth. Caravaggio swerves and its mouth rips open the boot to the right of his neck. Water is released. He feels himself becoming lighter. Being swung from side to side, no vision, no odour, he is ten years old and tilting wildly in a tree. A wall or an arm hits him. "Fucking wop! Fucking dago!" *"Honour your partner, dip and dive."* His hands are up squabbling with this water creature – sacrificing the hands to protect the body. The inside of his heart feels bloodless. He swallows dry breath. He needs more than anything to get on his knees and lap up water from a saucer.

Three men who have evolved smug and without race slash out. "Hello wop." And the man's kick into his stomach lets free the singer again as if a Wurlitzer were nudged, fast and flat tones weaving through a two-step as the men begin to beat the blindfolded Caravaggio. What allies with Caravaggio is only the singer, otherwise his mind is still caught underwater. Then they let him go.

He stands there still blindfolded, his hands out. The caller in the cell opposite quietens, knowing Caravaggio needs to listen within the silence for any clue as to where the men are. They are dumb beasts. He could steal the teeth out of their mouths. Everyone watches but him, eyes covered, hands out.

The homemade filed-down razor teeth swing in an arc to his

throat, to the right of the ripped-open boot. He drops back against the limestone wall. The other leather boot releases its cup-like hold on the water as if a lung gives up. A vacuum of silence.

He realizes the men have gone. The witness, the caller from the upper level, begins to talk quietly to him. "They have cut your neck. Do you understand! They have cut your neck. You must staunch it till someone comes." Then Patrick screams into the limestone darkness for help.

Caravaggio finds the bed. He gets to his knees on the mattress – head and elbows propping up his bruised body so nothing touches the pain. The blood flows along his chin into his mouth. He feels as if he has eaten the animal that attacked him and he spits out everything he can, old saliva, blood, spits again and again. Everything is escaping. His left hand touches his neck and it is not there.

*   *   *

The next morning Caravaggio explored the shoreline around the cottage in a canoe. He was out on the lake when a woman in another canoe emerged into the bay and hailed him. Red hair. The clear creamy skin of a witch. She wore a hat tied with a scarf and she waved to him in absolute confidence that if he was in a canoe on this lake he was acceptable and safe, even though every piece of clothing he wore was stolen from the blue bureau in the cottage. The lavender shirt, the white ducks, the tennis shoes. He stopped paddling. Performing intricate strokes, she pulled up alongside him.

– You are staying with the Neals.

– How did you know?

She gestured to the canoe. Here people recognized canoes.

    – Are they coming up for August?
    – I think so. They were unsure.
    – They always are. I'm Anne, a neighbour.

She pointed to the next property. She had on a bathing suit and a light skirt and was barefoot, the paddle resting on her shoulder.

    – I'm David.

Drops of water slid along the brown wood and onto her skin. He looked at her stunningly poreless face that now and then revealed itself out from the shadow of her straw hat. He decided to be direct about his tentative status.

    – I'm here to get my bearings.
    – This is a *good* place for that.

He looked up at her again, differently now, past the white creamy face and bare arms.

    – Why did you say it like that?

Her hand up to shield off the sun. A questioning look.

    – What you just said . . .
    – Just that I love this place. It can heal you if you are here alone. Are you an artist?
    – What?
    – You have aquamarine on your neck.

He smiled. He had spent so long calling it blue.

    – I should go, he said.

She lifted her paddle forward so it was across her knees, nodding to herself, realizing a wall had just been placed between them. Their canoes banged together and she backpaddled. He had never heard anyone speak as generously as she had in that one sentence. *This is a good place.*

– Thank you.

She turned, puzzled.

> – For pointing out the aquamarine.
> – Well . . . enjoy the lake.
> – I will.

She sensed his withdrawal. Alone, not having seen anyone for weeks, she had come too close, spoken too loudly. He watched the frailness of her back as she canoed away from him.

Caravaggio looked over the body of water as if it were human now, a creature on whose back he shifted. He did not think of approaches or exits, suddenly there could be only descent or companionship.

*   *   *

The first time Caravaggio had noticed Patrick Lewis gazing down from the opposite cell, he had simply waved and looked elsewhere. Most of Caravaggio's time in prison was spent in restless sleep. The night light of cells, the constant noise, made him nervous. The prisoner opposite who had tried to burn down the Muskoka Hotel was worse. He always sat up erect on the bed watching the movements below him. When Caravaggio returned from the hospital, his throat sewn up after the attack, Patrick was waiting for him. And when Caravaggio woke in pain suddenly the next afternoon, he turned to find the man's gaze reassuring him. Patrick had sat up there smoking precisely, moving his hand and cigarette fully away from his face when he blew the smoke out.

– Do you have a red dog? he asked Caravaggio a few days later.
– Russet, he whispered back.
– You're the thief, right?
– The best there is; that's why, as you can see, I'm here.
– Someone let you down, I suppose.
– Yes. The red dog.

He had trained as a thief in unlit rooms, dismantling the legs of a kitchen table, unscrewing the backs of radios and the bottoms of toasters. He would draw the curtains to block out any hint of streetlight and empty the kitchen cupboards, then put everything back, having to remember as he worked where all the objects were on the floor. Such pelmanism. While his wife slept he moved the furniture out of her bedroom and brought in the sofa, changed the pictures on the wall, the doilies on the bedside table.

In daylight he moved slowly as if conserving remnants of energy – a bat in post-coital flight. He would step into an upholstery shop to pick up a parcel for his wife and read the furniture, displacing in his mind the chairs through that window, the harvest table through the door at a thirty-degree angle veering right.

As a thief he had a sense of the world which was limited to what existed for twenty feet around him.

During his first robbery Caravaggio injured himself leaping from a second-storey window. He lay on his back with a cracked ankle on the Whitevale lawn, a Jeffreys drawing in his arms. He lay there as the family walked into the house and shrieked when they came upon the chloroformed dog. All the porch lights went on, the shadow of a tree luckily falling across him.

Two hours later he stumbled on a settlement of long barns, not certain what they were till he was gathered in the smell. A mushroom factory. Only the hallways and offices were lit, the long dormitories where the mushrooms were grown were in permanent darkness. He knew what he needed. In the main lobby were the helmets with battery lamps attached to them. Now it was almost dawn. A Sunday. He had a day without being disturbed. Later in the sunlight he cut open his boot and sock. He made a splint and strapped it with electrical tape. Worse than the pain was his hunger. He looked at his stolen drawing in the sunlight, the clean lines, the shaky signature.

Around dusk he hobbled across the road to a vegetable garden, pulled up a few carrots and dropped them into his shirt. He tried to catch a chicken but it sped up its walk and left him behind. He returned to the minimal light in the halls of the mushroom factory. He read the punch cards of the workers. *Salvatorelli, Mascardelli, Daquila, Pereira, De Francesca.* Most of them Italian, some Portuguese. Shifts from eight to four. He felt safer. In the office he looked through the drawers and cabinets.

He knew people who took shits on desks whenever they broke into office buildings but he wasn't one of them. It was, he was told, a formal act. Most amateur thieves could not control themselves. With all their discipline focused on the idea of robbery, there was no governor of the body. The act implied grossness, but the professional thief turned from this gesture to a medicinal clarity in his survey of the room. Detailed receipts memorized, key pages razor-bladed. At the centre of the symmetrical plot was this false act of madness.

When Caravaggio joined the company of thieves he was struck first of all by their courtesy. Even the shitters looked refined and wore half-moon glasses; they would have taken snuff but for the fact it would destroy their sense of smell. The cafés in the west end of Toronto were full of these men who had no work in the afternoons, who woke at noon and, after shaving, lunched with their friends. Caravaggio was welcomed into their midst and lectured with great conservatism on the art of robbery. Some were "displacers," some stole animals, some kidnapped dogs and wives, some would deal only in meat products or paper information. They were protective of their style and area of interest. They tried to persuade the young man that what *they* did was the most significant but at the same time they did not wish to encourage too much competition.

He was young. He was in awe of them, wanted to be all of them in their moments of extreme crisis. He hung around them not so much to learn their craft but to study the way they lived when they stepped back into the world of order. He still had that to learn. He was twenty-two at the Blue Cellar Café and he was fascinated only by character. He was a young man stepping into a mansion and being overcome with the generosity of envy. He slid his hand down the smoothness of a banister and his palm and fingers luxuriated in it. The intricate light switches! The carpets your feet melted into! He did this with their character – he walked away with their mannerisms and their brand names, the rhythm and abstract tone of their musings.

Later he trailed each of them for a week in order to watch their performances. Some of them went into houses and spent three hours and came out with objects so small they fit into a side pocket. Some removed every moveable object on the ground floor in half an hour.

And now, in the midst of his first robbery, Caravaggio read through the finances of the mushroom factory and came across a till of cash. Never steal where you sleep. All this inquiry was out of boredom. He wanted a book, he wanted meat. If he was going to have to hole up for a few days he wanted chicken and literature. Caravaggio switched on the light attached to the foreman's helmet and stepped into one of the mushroom dormitories he had selected earlier as his. Shelves at various levels ran the length of the long room. There were troughs on the shelves which held manure and earth and young growing mushrooms.

Now he was in a dark prison with millions of them. He snuggled into a space beneath the low shelf at the end farthest away from the door, his Jeffreys drawing beside him. He switched off the helmet, breathed in the thick vegetable air. He had not slept for a day and a half, had chloroformed his first dog, jumped out of a window, tried to race down a chicken . . .

Something brushed his face. Without opening his eyes he moved back. Earlier he had awakened with fragments of light above him as figures leaned over the troughs to select mushrooms. The mushrooms were grown at different stages, a few weeks apart, so there would always be a section ready. He had fallen back to sleep among the sounds of overalls rubbing against the shelves. Now the cloth against his face startled him. A woman on his right stood tentatively on one foot. She struggled with a shoe, leaning against the plaster wall in a slip, the upper half of her body naked. Her helmet balanced on the top shelf was facing her so she could see what she was doing as she dressed. Her black shadow moved parallel to her whiteness.

He remained still. Raven hair and an angular face, her body reaching up to pull down a blouse from a hook, more secure now with both shoes on.

— Psst.

She looked sternly out into darkness, picked up the helmet, and diverted light across the room through the shelves.

— Angelica? Is that you? she called out.

She pulled on her skirt with one hand holding the helmet, stopped, put the helmet on, and did up the buttons. She began singing to herself. He had to get her attention without terrifying her. He started humming along with her. Her helmet light came down fast to where he was and she lashed out, kicking his face. After a yell of pain he began to laugh.

— Please, tomorrow bring me something to eat.
— *Perchè?*
— I'm a thief. I've broken my ankle.

She bent down and put her hand out.

— *Tartufi?* What are you stealing? Mushrooms?

Her hands were on his foot, felt the ankle strapped up, and believed everything, knowing already he was gentle by his laugh.

— I broke it a mile or two from here. I'm very hungry. Please bring me some chicken tomorrow.

He could not see her face at all, just the hem of the skirt at her knees where the light bounced as she crouched. Now all he could know of her was a voice, confident, laughing with him.

– *Come si chiama?*
– Giannetta.
– I'm Caravaggio.
– A thief.
– *Sicuro.*
– I'll bring you some chicken tomorrow. And a bible.
– Let me see your face.
– *Basta! Ha visto abbastanza.*

She patted his foot.

– Do you need anything else?
– Ask what I should do about my ankle.

There was darkness again and he yearned for light. The thin beam from her helmet, the delicate ribs as she reached up for the blouse, her shadow overcoming his memory so he had to begin the scene again, a small loop of film, seven or eight seconds, until she reached for the lamp and put herself in darkness. He repeated it again and again and then turned to her voice. Strange how he wanted chicken above all else. It was that useless chase in the yard across the road, itching in his memory.

The next morning she arrived and asked him to turn his head while she changed. She told him how each of the workers chose a room or one corner for changing into and out of their overalls. She unwrapped a large cloth and gave him the food. Chicken and some salad and milk and banana cake. It was the worst banana cake he had eaten up to that point in his life.

– *Devo partire. Ritornerò.*

In the afternoon Giannetta and three other women workers came by to have a look at him. There were the expected jokes, but he enjoyed the company after so much solitude. When they left, noisily, she put her hand out. She touched his mouth gently. Then she brought out bandages and restrapped his ankle.

> – *Cosí va meglio.*
> – When can I get out of here?
> – We've planned something for you.
> – *Bene*. Let me see your face.

Her lamp remained still at his foot. So he reached back for his foreman's helmet and shone it on her. She remained looking down. He realized his right hand was still holding her ankle from when she had removed the electrical tape off him painfully.

> – Thank you for helping me.
> – I am sorry I kicked you so hard.

The next day Giannetta crouched beside him, smiling.

> – We must shave off your moustache. Only women work here.
> – *Mannaggia!*
> – We have to get you out as a woman.

He reached out his hand and put his fingers into her hair, into that darkness.

> – Giannetta.
> – You have to put your arm down.

Her hand rested at his shoulder, holding onto the straight razor. He would not let her go.

Their faces darkened as they leaned forward, her lamp shining past his head. He could smell her skin.

> — Here comes the first kiss, she whispered.

She handed him the dress.

> — *Non guardare*, please. Don't look.

He realized he was standing exactly where she had been a few days earlier. He switched on his lamp so it beamed onto her, then began to take off his shirt, paused, but she kept looking at him. He saw his own shadow on the wall. She came forward, smiling, calming his balance as he stood on his good foot.

> — Here, I'll show you how to put on a dress. Unbutton this first.

She held the cloth bunched over his nakedness.

> — Ahh Caravaggio, shall we tell our children how we met?

*   *   *

This time he did not take the canoe. He had already walked the shoreline before dusk, remembering the swamp patches. Now, dressed in dark clothes, he traced his path towards the compound belonging to the woman with the canoe — the main building, outlying cottages, a boathouse, an icehouse. He had no idea what the lake was called. He had passed a sign when he was running that claimed the area was Featherstone Point. That was when he saw the telephone wires which he knew must come from her group of houses.

He came through the last of the trees into the open area and everything was in darkness, as if the owners had packed up and left. He had expected to see rectangles of light. Now he lost all perspective and did not know how fully he would have to turn to be aimed back at his cottage. He needed some context of the human. A dog on a chain, a window, a sound. He turned once more and saw moonlight on the lake. But there was no moon. He realized it had to be light from the boathouse. The landscape, the blueprint of the compound, sprang back into his brain. He walked towards the water knowing where the low shrubs were, the stone hedge, the topiary he could not see. He slipped inside the boathouse and listened for sounds of activity. Nothing. With a pulley-chain used for hoisting up boat engines he swung up onto the first roof which was like a skirt around the upper cabin. He walked up the slope. The woman named Anne was sitting inside at a table.

Light from an oil lamp. She faced the water, her night window, and was writing hunched over the table unaware of anything else in the room. A summer skirt, an old shirt of her husband's, sleeves rolled up. She glanced up from the page and peered into the kerosene of the lamp. The mind behind the gaze did not know where it was. Caravaggio had never witnessed someone writing before. He saw her put down the fountain pen and later pick it up, try it, and realizing the nib was dry, lift the tail of her shirt to wipe the dry ink off the nib, preening the groove, as if the pause were not caused by the hesitation of her mind but by the atrophy of the pen. Now she bent over earnestly, half-smiling, the tongue moving in her mouth.

If she had turned to her right she would have seen his head at one of the small panes of glass, the light from the oil lamp just reaching it. He thought of that possible glance and moved back further. He thought of all those libraries he had stepped into in Toronto homes, the grand vistas of bookcases that reached the ceiling, the books of pigskin and other leathers that fell into his arms as he climbed up the shelves looking for whatever valuables he imagined were there, his boots pushing in the books to get a toe-hold. And then from up there, his head close to the ceiling, looking down on the rectangle of the rooms, hearing his dog's clear warning bark, not moving. And the door opening below him – a man walking in to pick up the telephone and dialling, while Caravaggio hung high up on the bookcases knowing now he should move the second he was seen up there in his dark trousers and singlet, as still as a gargoyle against Trollope and H.G. Wells. He could land on the leather sofa and bounce into the man's body before he even said a word into the phone. Then go through the French doors without opening them, a hunch of his body as he breaks through the glass and thin wood, then a blind leap off the balcony into the garden, where he would curse his dog for the late warning, and take off.

But this boathouse had no grandeur. The woman's bare feet rested one on top of the other on the stained-wood floor. A lamp on the desk, a mattress on the floor. In this light, and with all the small panes of glass around her, she was inside a diamond, mothlike on the edge of burning kerosene, caught in the centre of all the facets. He knew there was such intimacy in what he was seeing that not even a husband could get closer than him, a thief who saw this rich woman trying to discover what she was or what she was capable of making.

He put his hands up to his face and smelled them. Oil and rust. They smelled of the chain. That was always true of thieves, they smelled of what they brushed against. Paint, mushrooms, printing machines, yet they never smelled of the rich. He liked people who smelled of their trade – carpenters cutting into cedar, dog-catchers who carried the odour of wet struggling hounds with them. And what did this woman smell of? In this yellow pine room past midnight she was staring into a bowl of kerosene as if seeing right through the skull of a lover.

He was anonymous, with never a stillness in his life like this woman's. He stood on the roof outside, an outline of a bear in her subconscious, and she quarried past it to another secret, one of her own, articulated wet and black on the page. The houses in Toronto he had helped build or paint or break into were unmarked. He would never leave his name where his skill had been. He was one of those who have a fury or a sadness of only being described by someone else. A tarrer of roads, a house-builder, a painter, a thief – yet he was invisible to all around him.

He leapt through darkness onto the summer grass and then walked up to the main building. Without turning on lights he found the telephone in the kitchen and phoned his wife in Toronto.

> – Well I got out.
> – *Lo so.*
> – How?
> – The police were here. *Scomparso.* Not that you escaped but that you disappeared.
> – When did they come there?
> – Last week. A couple of days after you got away.
> – How's August?
> – He's with me. He misses his night walks.

She began to talk about her brother-in-law's house, which she had moved into. This time through a darkness which was distance.

> – I'll be back when I can, Giannetta.
> – Be careful.

She was standing in the centre of the living room in the darkness as he came away from the phone. His ear had been focused to Giannetta's voice, nothing else. His head imagining her – the alabaster face, the raven head.

> – *Non riuscivo a trovarti.*
> – Speak English.
> – I couldn't find you to ask.
> – You found the cottage, you found the phone, you could have found me.
> – I could have. It's a habit . . . usually I don't ask.
> – I'm going to light a lamp.
> – Yes, that's always safer.

She lifted the glass chimney and held the match to the wick. It lit up the skirt and shirt and her red hair. She moved away from it and leaned against the back of the sofa.

> – Where were you calling?
> – Toronto. My wife.
> – I see.
> – I'll pay for it.

She waved the suggestion away.

> – Is that your husband's shirt?
> – No. My husband's shirts are here, though. You want them?

He shook his head, looking around the room. A fireplace, a straight staircase, bedrooms upstairs.

– What do you want? You are a thief, right?
– With cottages all you can steal is the space or the people. I needed to use your phone.
– I'm going to eat something. Do you want some food?
– Thank you.

He followed her into the kitchen feeling relaxed with her – as if this was a continuation of his conversation with Giannetta.

– Tell me . . .
– David.
– David, why I am not scared of you?
– Because you've come back from someplace. . . . You got something there. Or you're still there.
– What are you talking about?
– I was on the roof of the boathouse. I did find you.
– I thought there was a bear around tonight.

She sits across from him laughing at the story of his escape, not fully believing it. A fairy tale. She cups her hand over the glass chimney and blows the lamp out. Two in the morning. As they go into darkness his mind holds onto the image of her slightness, the poreless skin, the bright hair leaning into the light. The startling colours of her strange beauty.

– I can't stand any more light, she says.
– Yes, this *is* the night. Allow the darkness in.
– I had to stay in a dark room once . . . with measles.

Her voice is exact, crystal clear. He has his eyes closed, listening to her.

– I was a kid. My uncle – he's a famous doctor – came to see me. In my room, all the blinds were down, the lights drowned. So I could do nothing. I wasn't allowed to read. He said I've brought you earrings. They are special earrings. He pulled out some cherries. Two, joined by their stalks, and he hung them over one ear and took out another pair and hung them over the other ear. That kept me going for days. I couldn't lie down at night without carefully taking them off and laying them on the night table.

– Do you have any children?

– I have a son. He comes up with my husband in a day or so. I have a brother who doesn't speak. This is his shirt. He hasn't spoken for years.

Caravaggio lies on the carpet. He had, when there was light earlier, been looking up at the tongue and groove, theorizing how one removed such floors. She continues talking.

– In a few days all the husbands come to the lake. A strange custom. I've been so happy these last three weeks. Listen . . . no sound. In the boathouse there is always the noise of the lake. I feel bereaved when the lake is still, mute.

There is now a silence in the room. He stands up.

– I should go.

– You can sleep on the sofa.

– No. I should go.

– You can sleep here. I'm going up to bed.

– I'm a *thief*, Anne, *un ladro*.

– That's right. You broke out of jail.

He sees her clearly on the other side of the unlit lamp, her chin on her clenched fist.

> – I have literally fallen in love with the lake. I dread the day I will have to leave it. Tonight I was writing the first love poem I have written in years and the lover was the sound of lakewater.
> – I've always had a fear of water creatures.
> – But water is benign . . .
> – Yes, I know. Goodbye, Anne.

*　　*　　*

After his marriage to Giannetta, Caravaggio had one pit to fall into before his career as a thief became successful – he was overwhelmed suddenly by a self-consciousness. He broke into houses and became certain there was a plot concocted to snare him. Giannetta could not stand it. She did not wish to live with a well-trained thief who feared going out.

> – Get a partner!
> – I can never work with someone else, you know that!
> – Then get a dog!

He stole a dark-red fox terrier and named it August. A summer robbery. The dog was his salvation. He had a quick bark, like an exclamation – one announcement, take it or leave it – enough warning for his master as far as the dog was concerned.

On a job they behaved like strangers – Caravaggio strolling along one side of the street and August aimless on the other.

When he entered a house the dog sat on the lawn. If the owners returned early the dog would stand up and give one clear bark. Moments later a figure would leap from a window with a carpet or a suitcase in his arms.

*   *   *

Now he pours milk into the tall glass and drinks as he walks through his brother-in-law's house, the coolness of milk filling him on this hot Toronto night. He is seated on the stairs, facing the door. He hears the dog's one clear bark and her laugh as she approaches the front door.

In the dark hall the whiteness of the milk disappears into his body. Her shoulders nestle against his hands. The home of the other. Touching her, a wetness passed from her lip to him, his hands in her dark hair. She moves within the shadow of his shoulder.

She steps into the half-lit kitchen and her bare arms pick up light. He catches the blink of her earrings. Removing one, she drops it to the floor. Her hands go up to the other ear – unscrewing the second pin of gold. Her laughter with her breast in his mouth.

He breaks the necklace and pearls fall around them. He can smell soaps in her hair. Her wrist moves up his arm, riding on the sweat. Her cheek against the warm tile. Her other hand, sweeping out, touches the loose jewel.

Giannetta feels the scar on his throat. Her soft kiss across it. He carries her, still in her, holding up each thigh, her eyes wide open, crockery behind her crashing from shelf to shelf, as she nudges the corner cupboard. Blue plates bounce and come through the lower panes like water and smash on the floor.

With each step her bare foot on a pearl or a fragment of plate. She opens the fridge door. In its light she pulls her foot up to her stomach and examines it, brushing something away. He lies back and she sits over him, swallowing the cold wine. He traces the path down her body at the speed he imagines liquid takes.

Her chin on her knee. Planting her foot on his shoulder she leaves blood when she moves it. When she opens her eyes wide he sees glass and crockery and thin china plates tumbling down from shelf to shelf losing their order, their shades of blue and red merging, her fingers on his scar, her fingers on the thumping vein on his forehead. She's a laugher who laughs while they make love, not earnest like a tightrope-walker.

Her low laugh when they stop, exhausted.

His breath is now almost whisper, almost language. She turns, a pearl embedded in her flesh. A violin with stars walking in this house. Fridge light sink light street light. At the sink she douses her face and shoulders. She lies beside him. The taste of the other. A bazaar of muscles and flavours. She rubs his semen into his wet hair. Her shoulders bang against the blue-stained cupboard. A kitchen being fucked. Sexual portage. Her body forked off him.

She smells him, the animal out of the desert that has stumbled back home, back into oasis. Her black hair spreads like a pool over the tiles. She pins the earring her fingers had strayed upon into his arm muscle, beginning a tattoo of blood.

There are jewels of every colour he has stolen for her in the past in the false drawers of her new bedroom, which he can find by ripping out the backs of the bureaus. Photographs of her relatives in old silver frames. A clock encased in glass which turns its gold stomach from side to side to opposite corners of the room. A wedding ring he can pull off her finger with his teeth.

He removes nothing. Only the chemise she withdraws from as if skin. He carries nothing but the jewellery pinned to his arm, a footstep of blood on his shoulder. The feather of her lip on his mouth.

A last plate tips over to the next shelf. He waits for her eye to open. Here comes the first kiss.

All she can see as she enters the dark hall is the whiteness of the milk, a sacred stone in his hands, disappearing into his body.

He lifts his wife onto his shoulders so her arms ascend into the chandelier.

MARITIME THEATRE

I N 1938, WHEN Patrick Lewis was released from prison, people were crowding together in large dark buildings across North America to see Garbo as Anna Karenina. Everyone tried to play the Hammond Organ. 'Red Squads' intercepted mail, teargassed political meetings. By now over 10,000 foreign-born workers had been deported out of the country. Everyone sang "Just One of Those Things." The longest bridge in the world was being built over the lower Zambesi and the great waterworks at the east end of Toronto neared completion.

At Kew Park a white horse dove every hour from a great height into Lake Ontario. T.S. Eliot's *Murder in the Cathedral* opened in England and a few weeks later Dr. Carl Weiss – who had always admired the poetry of the expatriate American – shot Huey Long to death in the Louisiana capitol building. Just one of those things.

Released from prison in January, he took the Kingston train to Toronto's Union Station. *Ten Story Gang*, *Weird Tales*, *Click*, *Judge Sheard's Best Jokes*, and *Look* were in the magazine stalls. Patrick sat down on the smooth concrete bench facing the ramp down to the gates. This cathedral-like space was the nexus of his life. He had been twenty-one when he arrived in this city. Here he had watched Clara leave him, walking past that sign to the left of the ramp which said HORIZON. *Look up*, Clara had said when she left him for Ambrose, *you know what that stone is?* He had been lost in their situation, not caring. *It's*

Missouri Zumbro. Remember that. The floors are Tennessee marble. He looked up. Sitting now on this bench Patrick suddenly had no idea what year it was.

He brought Clara's face directly back into memory – as if it were a quizzical smiling face on a poster advertising a hat to strangers. But Alice's face, with its changeability, he could not evoke. A group of redcaps were standing with three large cages full of dogs, all of whom were barking like aristocrats claiming to be wrongly imprisoned. He went up to the cages. They were anxious with noise. He had come from a place where a tin cup against a cell wall was the sole form of protest. He got closer to the cages, looked into the eyes which saw nothing, the way his own face in prison had looked in a metal mirror.

He was still crouched when the redcaps wheeled the cages down the ramp. On his knees in Union Station. He felt like the weight on the end of a plumb-bob hanging from the very centre of the grand rotunda, the absolute focus of the building. Slowly his vision began to swing. He turned his head to the left to the right to the left, discovering the horizon.

He moved tentatively into the city, standing in front of strangers, studying the new fashions. He felt invisible. Outside Union Station the streets were deep in snowdrifts. He walked towards the east end, along Eastern Avenue, till he eventually came to the Geranium Bakery, entering the warm large space where winter sun pierced through the mist of flour in the air. He passed the spotless machines, looking for Nicholas. Buns moved forward along rollers till they were flipped over into the small lake of sizzling shortening. Finally he saw him in his suit covered with white dust at the far end of the bakery, choreographing the movement of food. Nicholas Temelcoff walked forward and embraced him. A bear's grip. The grip of the world.

– Welcome back, my friend.

– Is she here?

Nicholas nodded.

– She has packed her things.

Patrick climbed into the service elevator and pulled the rope beside him which took him up to Nicholas' living quarters on the next floor. He went in and knocked on the door of the small room.

Hana was sitting on the bed wearing a frock, her hands on her lap. Looking down, then up slowly, the way Alice used to glance up, the eyes moving first. So much like Alice it was terrible to him. He turned away and looked at the girl's neat room, at the packed suitcase, the light on beside her bed in the daylight.

She watched him, understanding what kind of love was behind his stare. His cheek was pressed against the door frame, the new jacket collar rough against his neck. Five years earlier, before he had taken the train to the Muskokas, they had come to the Geranium Bakery. And Nicholas had offered to look after her. She was welcome to stay with his family. He had suggested this casually and with no hesitation, sitting in his office under the clock Hana loved, where each hour was represented by a different style of doughnut. *"Each of us is on our own for a while now,"* Patrick had said. *"I know."* She had been eleven years old then.

She rose from the bed. "Hey, Patrick, look how tall I've got!" Stepping forward towards him and embracing him quietly, her arms all the way around him, the top of her head just reaching his chin.

At the Balkan Café they sat down and ordered *sujuk*, the sausages with leeks and pork and garlic that he had not eaten for so long.

– Are you healthy?

– Oh yes. As a horse.

– Good.

– I'll have to get used to things, though.

– That's okay, Patrick . . . and being in jail's okay too. Don't let it go to your head, though.

– No.

He felt comfortable joking with her, gathering her perspective. In prison when he imagined freedom it was as a solitary. Nothing to carry, nothing to fall back into the arms of. This was the image he luxuriated in, awake all night, watching the other prisoners turning like great grey fish in their cells. In prison he had protected himself with silence – as if any sentence would be unsafe territory, as if saying even one word would begin a release of Alice out of his body. Secrecy kept him powerful. By refusing communication he could hold her within himself, in his arms. But on the night Caravaggio was attacked, his father's neutral song slid out as warning. And Patrick turned from himself.

– Did you make any friends in prison? Hana asked.

– I made one friend. He escaped.

– Too bad. What did *he* do?

– He was a thief. Some people tried to cut his throat in jail.

– Then he's lucky he escaped.

– He was most clever.

Ambrose Small, as a millionaire, had always kept the land-scapes of his world separate, high walls between them. Lovers, compatriots, businessmen, were anonymous to each other. As far as they knew there were no others, or they assumed the others lived in far countries.

When Clara Dickens joined Ambrose Small after he eva-porated from the world of financial power she thought she would see the vista of his nature. But during the years that she lived with Ambrose she would know him only as he wanted to be known by her. There was no other road towards him. She was too close to him now – to his new daily obsessions, his tem-porary charm. She wanted to climb above him even once and gaze down, see the horizon that held him together.

What she discovered in the end – when he sat on the floor of the emptied room in Marmora, nothing else around him but Clara and the walls and the wood floor and the curtainless windows so he could sleep at night neatly within the coffin of moonlight – was much worse.

In the days before he died, Small's mind slipped free of its compartments as if what had kept all his diverse worlds separate had been pulled out of him like a spine. So as he talked and muttered towards Clara, events fell against each other – a night with a lover, a negotiation at the Grand Opera House. Strangers and corpses of his past arrived in this sparse room with its one lamp lit during the day, so the shadows were like moon-tides around it.

Words fell from his mouth and shocked her in the intricacy of his knowledge of so many women, such deep interiors of the financial sea. She heard his varied portraits of her which had gone unspoken for years, his affections and passions and irritations and reversals, his sweet awe at her sense of colour with certain flowers, the memory of her standing in a hall years earlier and smelling each of her armpits when she thought she was alone.

Clara crouched in front of Ambrose and now he could not see her. He was sitting lotus, bare-chested, his hands moving over his face sensuously rubbing the front of his skull, as he revealed the mirrors of himself, his voice slowing as his fingers discovered his right ear. Then he bent forward as he sat so his head would touch the floor in a long grace-attempted bow, ascetic. A heron stretching his head further underwater, the eyes open within the cold flow, open for the fish that could then be raised into the air and dropped moving in the tunnel of the heron's blue throat.

She sat on the floor, ten feet away from Ambrose, the lamp beside her, attacked by all the discontinuous moments of his past. Who were these women? Where did those destroyed enemies go? Ambrose spoke slowly, the uninterested words came from his dark, half-naked shape as if all this was just the emptying of pails to be free of ballast. The theatres, his wife, his sisters, the women, enemies, Briffa, even Patrick, spilled free.

The only clarity for him now was this bare room where Clara brought him food. He had imploded, had become a Gothic child suddenly full of a language which was aimed nowhere, only out of his body. Bitten flesh and manicures and greyhounds and sex and safe-combinations and knowledge of suicides. She saw his world as if she were tied to a galloping horse, caught glimpses of faces and argument and there was no horizon. After all these years she would not be satisfied, would not know him. She pulled back.

Now his face serene. Now his upper torso bent forward long and athletic and the mouth of the heron touched the blue wood floor and his head submerged under the water and pivoted and saw in the fading human light a lamp that was the moon.

The girl was shaking him from side to side as he slept in the kitchen chair, in the apartment on Albany Street. Fragments of lobster were scattered across the table.

> – Patrick! Patrick! You've got to wake up.
> – What . . .
> – It's urgent. I don't know how I forgot but I forgot. Wake up, Patrick, please. She was going to wait. I don't know how I forgot.
> – What is it?
> – Someone called Clara Dickens. She's on the phone.
> – What is this? Where am I?
> – It's important, Patrick.
> – I'm sure it is.
> – Can you get to the phone?
> – Yup. You go to bed.

He put his face under the kitchen tap. Clara Dickens. After a hundred years.

He stood there breathing deeply. He walked into the dark room, his face still wet, and got to his knees. One arm was in a cast and he reached out the other hand feeling for the telephone. "Don't hang up. Don't hang up," he was yelling, hoping she could hear him until he found the telephone.

— This is Patrick.

— I know who it is.

He heard her half-laugh at the other end.

— Who was that who answered the phone?

— A friend. You've never met her.

— That's good.

— She's sixteen, Clara, I'm looking after her.

— I'm in Marmora. Will you come and get me?

Ambrose is dead.

He was silent, lying on his back in a dark room. He knew this room well in the dark. He had been here often.

— You take Highway 7 . . . are you there? I need help, Patrick.

He could see the swirls in the ceiling.

— Have I been to Marmora?

— It's four hours from Toronto. It's supposedly the sled-dog capital of Ontario. I'm calling from a restaurant. I've been here for four hours.

— Four hours! What year is it?

— Don't be cynical, Patrick. Not now, okay?

— Describe where you are, the place you are standing in. I just need to hear you.

— I've been outside, sitting next to one of those artificial negro fishermen you see all over the place nowadays. It was damn cold. I phoned about ten. You were supposed to call back.

— She forgot. She got excited because I brought home a lobster. But now we have goddamn *deus ex machina.* You're on the phone. Did Ambrose get shot with a silver bullet?

– He died of natural causes.

– Run over by a sled-dog, was he?

At this he couldn't stop laughing and turned from the phone. He could hear her voice, tinny in the distance.

– I'm sorry, he said.

– No, that's probably funny. Want to hear more?

– Yes.

– I've read the *Marmora Herald* pretty thoroughly.

– You're not carrying a book?

– That's right. I forgot you're the man who taught me to always carry a book. . . . What are you doing?

– I'm lying in the dark. I'll come and get you, Clara.

– Will you be okay? The girl said you have a broken arm.

– I'll bring her with me. She'll keep me awake. She's very earnest about things like that.

– The kind of woman you always wanted.

– That's right. She saved my life.

– Are you her father, Patrick?

– What's the name of the restaurant?

– "Heart of Marmora."

– Give us about five hours or so. I need a short rest . . . wait. Are you there?

– Yes.

– I am her father.

He rose and went to Hana's room. He felt exhausted.

– Who is she, Patrick?

– Hana, I need you to come with me, to drive up to Marmora.

– The sled-dog capital of Ontario?

– What? . . . *What!*

She was beaming.

– She told me, Patrick, when I asked her where the call was coming from. We're going all the way there to pick her up?

– Yeah.

She stood by the door, watching him, wanting him to say more.

– How the hell did she end up there . . .

– Was she running away from you?

– I think so . . . with another man anyway. I need a little sleep first. Wake me in about forty minutes.

– Sure. You going to tell me about her on the drive?

– Yes.

– Great!

When Patrick had come out of prison six months earlier many dissident groups were already voicing themselves within the city. The events in Spain, the government's crackdown on unions, made the rich and powerful close ranks. Troops were in evidence everywhere. When the last shift left the water-filtration plant the police and the army moved in to guard it. Military tents bivouacked on the rolling grounds. There were soldiers on the roofs and searchlights dipped now and then along the waves of the lake, protecting against any possible attack from the direction of the lakeshore. While most public buildings were guarded, the waterworks was obsessively watched – partly because of the warnings of Commissioner Harris, who reminded officials that the Goths could have captured Rome by destroying the aqueducts which led into the city. Cutting off the water supply or poisoning it would bring the city to its knees.

Harris saw the new building as a human body. For him there were six locations where it could be seriously crippled – the raw water pumps, the Venturi meters, the entrance to the tanks where ferric chloride was poured, the twenty-four-foot-deep settling basins, and any one of the twenty filter pools where an explosion would cause floods and permanently rust all engines and electrical equipment. There was also the intake-pipe tunnel that ran almost a mile and a half out into the lake. No boats were allowed within a half-mile of the shoreline and no one, not even military personnel, was admitted into the building at night. Only Harris, who now insisted on sleeping there in his office, was allowed in, a pistol kept beside his bed.

In his dressing-gown, at two in the morning, Commissioner Harris was happy in the cocoon of humming machines. He would get up and roam through the palace of water which he had dreamed and desired and built. Every electrical outlet blazed, lighting up disappearing corridors as if Viennese streets, turning the subterranean filter pools into cloudy ballrooms. The building pulsed all night in the east end of the city on the edge of Lake Ontario. It was rumoured that people on the south shore in New York State could see the aura from it.

The filtration plant was one corner of a triangle of light that seemed to chart the city on this Saturday night in the summer of 1938. Another was a river of lights moving north up Yonge Street from the lake. And third was the dazzle from the Yacht Club on Toronto Island – holding its summer costume ball, with water taxis ferrying bizarrely dressed society across the bay on the one-mile trip over rough water.

Such dance floors the rich spent their evenings on! Strutting like colts in a warm barn, out of the rain. And in bed the following morning they would reconstruct the choreography of temptations which had carried them from the crowded periphery of the hall to the sprung dance floor beneath the thirty-foot coconut palms – clusters of which adorned the ballroom that seemed to have no ceiling, only false stars and false moonlight. In each set of trees was a live monkey, never able to reach the diners because of a frail chain. The animals had to dodge the champagne corks aimed at them – if you hit a monkey you were brought a free bottle. Sales of champagne soared and only now and then was there a shriek followed by a cheer.

There was a silk canopy over the band. Along the walls were

dioramas. Sometimes cotton snowballs were distributed and a battle broke out promptly, the guests soaking them in champagne or butter before flinging them around the room. The ballroom was lit indirectly; it seemed they were all in a moment of time that resembled the half-hour before the sun comes up over an oasis.

There is an image of Caravaggio among the rich which Patrick will always remember: meticulous, rude, and confident. A parting in his dark hair like Yonge Street at midnight. Dressed as a pirate, he had leapt off the motor launch on that midsummer night with his dog and Giannetta and Patrick, yelled his greetings to total strangers, and strolled into the false moonlight of the Yacht Club ballroom claiming to be Randolph Frog. Society women accepted his name with a straight face – the rich, being able to change everything but their names and looks, would defend these characteristics with care. In this circle a man with the face of a pit bull was considered distinguished.

They had not been invited. Caravaggio was eating canapés with his left hand and patting women on the ass with his right. When the orchestra's playing brought out the couples, Caravaggio lifted his dog into his arms and waltzed among them kissing August wildly, exclaiming over the beauty of his moles. For the next hour he danced with women who noted to themselves the odour of hound on his neck. Patrick and Giannetta meanwhile hung back on the periphery of the ballroom, refusing to leave it as if they might fall into a snakepit. But Caravaggio was a man who had traipsed through the gardens and furnishings of the wealthy for many years. He nudged men, told jokes, discussed china and crystal with wives and connoisseurs, complaining about getting Louis XIV chairs cleaned, and in the privacy behind his drunkenness cemented away information and addresses.

Finally he found the couple he wanted. In their early forties, drinking hard, a flirtatious wife and a bully of a husband. He danced with his eyes against hers singing "Night and Day."

> *"Vicina o lontana da me*
> *non importa mia cara, dove sei . . ."*

She was impressed by his Italian, which he claimed to have picked up in Tuscany the previous summer. His fingers circled her shoulder blade. She leaned back.

    – Do you see my husband over there near the chandelier propositioning that girl? He's probably suggesting the yacht.
    – A yacht here?
    – Yes, we came in one, across the bay. Did you?
    – No. I never sail.
    – We'll take you.

He laughed, dropping a half-smoked cigarette onto the floor.

    – That's my shy sister over there.

She glanced across the room to the hollow glare of Giannetta, who held on to Patrick's arm.

    – Perhaps she could join us too.

Taking the bus down to the dock earlier that evening, Caravaggio had said, "Let me tell you about the rich – they have a way of laughing." And Patrick thought, Alice had said that. The exact words. "The only thing that holds the rich to the earth is property," Caravaggio continued, "their bureaus, their marble tables, their jewellery. . . ." Patrick had been quiet, not even bothering to laugh.

    There was an image he remembered of Caravaggio, waving

goodbye with a blue hand as he hung on the prison roof. And when Patrick had come out of jail he traced the thief down through his Blue Cellar compatriots. "Mr. Wilful Destruction of Property saved my life," Caravaggio had explained to Giannetta. They showed him the city, where everything was five years older, and they became his friends. Late into those spring nights they had talked about each other's lives.

On reconnaissance the week before the Yacht Club dance, Giannetta had watched Patrick get drunk, and during the ride back on the ferry she had held him, his head in her lap. She leaned over him in the darkness, her hand in his hair. He looked up. There was a tenderness in this sky of her warm face he hadn't noticed before. Then everything had leapt from focus as Giannetta and Caravaggio lifted him off the ferry and brought him home to sleep on their living-room floor.

Now they step from the last stages of the costume ball out onto the dock: Caravaggio, his two rich friends, his dog, his 'sister,' and Patrick, who is supposedly her escort for the evening.

> "... notte e giorno
> Questo ... mmm ...
> mi segue ovunque io vada"

Caravaggio sings to the night, a bottle like a pendulum in his fingers, his arm sprawled over the woman's shoulder. He pours out monologues about cut glass and bevelled mirrors and rubs her nipple to the beat of his singing as her husband unlaces the boat from its moorings. Patrick walks behind dressed as a thief in black, a red scarf floating behind him and carrying a bag of tools with SWAG written across it.

Boarding the couple's yacht, *The Annalisa*, Caravaggio flings himself down the stairs laughing, looking for alcohol. He is beyond order. He and the husband uncork several bottles and climb back up on deck. The wife winds up the gramophone, the silk dress with a thousand sequins fluttering upon her. Giannetta leans against the rail receiving the air while the husband unleashes the sails and they break loose out into the bay – from the island towards the city. Bunny Berigan pierces the air with his trumpet whirling up in scales, leaving the orchestras of the Yacht Club behind. They are off. Rich.

Caravaggio claims helplessness with ropes and asks the wife to dance. He is charmed by her flippant sexuality. They fumble against each other with the motion of the waves, Giannetta and Patrick somewhere by the prow. The boat tacks back and forth towards the city a mile away. Caravaggio and the husband and the wife drink fast. The wife winds up the gramophone and "I Can't Get Started" emerges again under the hiss of the needle.

Caravaggio catches Patrick's eye and raises his glass. "Here's to impatience," he toasts, "here's to H.G. Wells," then flings his glass overboard. It is a hot night and he removes his cloak. The woman touches his costume earrings with her fingernails. *Ting.* "Ting," she mouths at him. "Are you hungry?"

Down below she opens the fridge door. He sits and swivels in the chair round and round passing the blur of her salmon-coloured dress, the drink spilling from his glass. He rotates to a halt and she is there by the fridge holding ice against her face for the heat, unhooking the brooch at her shoulder so a part of the dress falls revealing a doorway of skin to one side of her. The smell from the gas lamp beside him fills his head. He puts all his effort into his shoulders and bends forward so he can get up out of the chair and stand. Now he must be still. Music everywhere. He starts laughing. Can a man lose his balance with an erection? Deep thoughts. He turns to face her. Dear

Salmon. She steps forward to hold him. His cheek on the moist skin under her arm, at the rib, about where they pierced Jesus he thinks. He falls drunkenly to his knees. He holds her dress at the thighs as she slips down, slips through the dress so there is a bunched sequin sheath in his hands. The music ceases. A serious pause. They jerk with the swell of waves and he holds her hair from the back. He pulls his handkerchief out of his pocket and in direct light brings it to her face and chloroforms her.

Patrick's hand comes round the large face in the night air and chloroforms the husband.

Caravaggio is on the floor of the hold, the unconscious woman in his arms, the dress around her waist. She dreams of what? he wonders. He lies there comfortable against her, in the silence left by Giannetta's hand lifting the needle off the record. He slides from under her, looks around, puts a blanket on top of her, and goes up on deck.

The husband lies nestled in the ropes. In his tuxedo he looks like a prop, a stolen mannequin. Above him, balanced on the rail of the boat, Patrick stands and pisses into the waves. Caravaggio mans the boat as Giannetta turns out the deck lights. "Is this the prow?" Patrick yells. "Am I pissing off the prow? Or bow?" Giannetta laughs. "I better get you ready." "Yes," he says. He walks to the back of the boat, scoops up the gramophone, and flings it overboard.

Caravaggio aims the yacht towards the east end of the city, towards the lights of Kew Park and the waterworks. Patrick and Giannetta go below deck. He takes some food out of the fridge, steps past the unconscious woman, and sits at the table. He is like a bullet that has been sleeping. That is how he has felt all night, in the slipstream of Caravaggio, fully relaxed, calm among his two friends. They have stopped him from thinking ahead. He wants the heart of the place. He wants to step in and destroy meticulously, efficiently. This is not to be a gesture of an egg hurled against a train window.

*　　*　　*

Throughout the night the giant intake pipe draws water into the filtration plant at a speed faster than during the day. Patrick knows that. From the plans Caravaggio has stolen for him, he knows its exact length, slightly under two miles, knows its angle and grade, knows the diameter of the pipe and the roughness of the metal inside and the narrower bands where the sections have been riveted together. He knows all the places he should assault once he is in the building.

On deck Giannetta watches Patrick, a small lantern beside them, the only light on the boat. He takes off his shirt and she begins to put grease onto his chest and shoulders. He watches her black hair as she rubs this darkness onto his body. The sweat on her collarbone. Her serious face. She suddenly leans forward and he feels her mouth briefly on his cheek. Then she pulls her head back into mystery and smiles at him, covering his face with the thick oil. When Caravaggio joins them, carrying the heavy SWAG bag, Patrick is ready. Giannetta embraces Caravaggio. With her fingers she plucks a sequin out of the darkness of his hair. Then the men climb down into the rowboat, absolute blackness around them. Only the filtration plant blazes on the shore a half-mile away. They pull free as Giannetta veers the yacht away, back towards the island.

Now the two men sit facing each other, knees touching. They are twenty or thirty yards from the floating structure where the intake pipe begins. "This is a charm," Caravaggio says, putting a metal spile attached to a leather thong around Patrick's neck. Caravaggio begins to dress Patrick with water-resistant dynamite – wrapping the sticks tightly against his chest under the thin black shirt. They both wear dark trousers. Patrick is invisible except by touch, grease covering all unclothed skin, his face, his hands, his bare feet. *Demarcation.* Caravaggio can sense his body, can feel and distinguish the belt straps, the button-locks that secure the fuses. The floating structure has sentries. They see lit cigarettes as they row towards them, Caravaggio leaning forward to touch Patrick's right arm to gesture him right, his left to gesture him left. No words. Only Caravaggio it seems can see into the weak spots of this absolute.

He attaches the tank onto Patrick's shoulders. Just one tank. They have estimated the speed of the water and the length of the tunnel. He could travel its distance in twelve minutes, but there is one risk. At some point in the night, pump generators are switched and for three minutes there is no suction at all. Then the water in the pipe does not move, it lies still. It would be the effect of a moving sidewalk stopping. They both know this could happen, have imagined Patrick no longer caught in the speed of the intake but languid, in a shock of stillness. The tank gives him only fifteen minutes of air. If the suction pump is off, the level of water in the normally full pipe might recede for a while and Patrick could possibly move to the top and breathe the air there. Neither of them is sure about this.

Just below the tank Caravaggio straps on the blasting-box and plunger. Small, brown, the maximum size Patrick can carry in order to get through the iron bars at the mouth of the intake pipe, which is there to stop logs and dead bodies from being drawn in. An animate body can squeeze through. In one of Patrick's nightmares while waiting for this evening he has imagined that in the pipe somewhere is a dead body which has magically slipped in and that he will clutch it during his journey.

At the far end of the tunnel is another barrier of iron bars which he will have to squeeze through. Then he will enter a forty-foot well where just above the water level will be a metal screen to keep out small objects and fish when the water is made to rise. He has the wire-cutters to get through this. Then he will be among the grey machines of the waterworks.

Caravaggio straps the battery lamp onto Patrick's head, then he embraces him. *"Auguri, amico mio."*

Patrick nods, puts the mouthpiece of the breathing apparatus between his lips, and rolls out of the boat. He holds on, treading water. Caravaggio leans over and switches on the lamp. They have choreographed this carefully for they knew there would be men near the entrance to the intake pipe. As the light goes on Patrick drives his head under water and his body follows downwards in an arc.

This is July 7, 1938. A night of no moon, a heat-wave in the city. The lemon-coloured glare from the waterworks delineates the east end. Caravaggio could lean forward and pluck it like some jewel from the neck of a negress. He rows in a straight line towards the waterworks, knowing Patrick is underneath him in the five-foot-diameter pipe racing within the current, his movement under water like a clenching fist, doubling up and releasing to full length, then doubling up, awkward because of the weight he carries.

In all of his imagining Caravaggio sees Patrick move with the light glancing wildly against the sides of the pipe. Whereas Patrick, having crawled through the iron bars, nearly unable to because of the tank, having done that and begun to swim, has discovered the lamp slows him too much so within seconds he has discarded it and it sinks to the foot of the pipe, the light still on, burning out an hour later. Patrick swims in darkness, just the pull of the water to guide him, clenching and releasing like that fist Caravaggio imagines, but banging his legs and hands against the sides of the pipe, doing this so often they are already bleeding from the blows and scrapes. Grease moves from his hair down his cheeks into his mouth. Most of all his body fears no air if the tank runs out, and the danger of silence among the pumps a mile away so he will suddenly move only at human speed. These fears are greater than the fear of no light or the remembered nightmare where he embraces the lost corpse. So his body, moving without thought, listens for silence. If the pumps stop, Caravaggio has told him to dynamite the pipe and climb out, leap from the water and yell. He will be there. But both know there is little chance of climbing out of that gashed metal while the whole lake pours in.

The searchlights from the filtration plant glance over the water. Now Caravaggio has to leave Patrick. He changes direction and rows towards Kew Beach a half-mile further west. The lights of the amusement park are slowly being turned off, past midnight. The outline of the Ferris wheel disappears.

Patrick swallows the first flutter of the dying tank.

He heaves faster along with the current and he takes deeper breaths from the tank. In the middle of the third breath he crashes against bars. He is almost there. Gasping, the mouth-piece dry, empty, torn out of his mouth. He is almost there with an empty tank. Now he needs the light. He slips off the tank, an arm painful from the crash, and dives through the bars and swings up, no air in him, no light, up into the brick of the well, avoiding the suction of the side-screens built into the walls. If these catch his body fully the suction can hold him and never release him. He swims up by feel till he reaches the barrier screen. Thinking where should he go, down again? How to get up further? For precious seconds, his chest vacuumed and almost imploded before he realizes he is *in* air. His shoulders and head and forearms are in the delicious air. This is the screen he is supposed to cut himself through. He can breathe if he opens his mouth. He is in the natural air of the waterworks.

He hangs, his fingers hooked through the wires of the screen, everything below his waist in water. The wire-cutters must have fallen in the crash against the bars or when he unstrapped the tank. For a while he doesn't care. He has air now. He knows he can never fight his way back against the current, down to the foot of the well. He is caught.

He hangs from one arm. A very small explosion to dislodge the firmly riveted screen and he will be out. He has five detonators. Sacrifice one location. How *small* an explosion can someone make? He attaches a blasting cap to the screen with a clip fuse, sets it off, and dives down as far as he can go. He does not hear the sound at all, he is just picked up and flung hard against the brick and then sucked upwards in a hunched ball with the water towards the buckled screen so his back and face are lacerated. Then he falls back down. There has been no sound for him, just movement, sideways and up, skin coming off his cheek and his back. There was, he remembers, temporary light. He can taste blood if he puts his tongue outside his mouth. And he can taste blood which comes down his nose through the roof of his mouth.

Patrick climbs out of the well and stands on the floor of the screen room among the grey machines, touching them to see if any are hot, a faint light from the main pumping station coming through a high window. He begins unwrapping the sticks of dynamite from his body and lays them in a row on the floor. Finding some cloth he wipes them dry. He removes from his pockets fuses, crimpers, timers, and detonator caps, which are wrapped in oil cloth. He unwinds the electrical wire and begins to assemble the blasting-box and plunger.

Stripping completely naked he squeezes the water out of his clothes and lays his shirt and pants against the hot machines. He lies down now and tries to rest. Trying to control his breathing, even now he desires to take large gasps in case this will be his last air. *King Solomon's Mines.* He smiles up in the darkness.

Harris, half-asleep on the makeshift bed in his office, has heard the thump, one thump that didn't fit into the pattern of noises made by the row of water pumps. He walks onto the mezzanine of the pumping station. It is brilliantly lit and stark. In his dressing-gown he descends the stairs to the low-level pumping station, walks twenty-five yards into the Venturi tunnels, and then returns slowly, listening again for that false thump. He has seen nothing but the grey-painted machines. On the upper level he looks out of the windows and sees the military patrols. He relaxes and goes back to his room.

Patrick rests without closing his eyes, his gaze on the high window that brings light into this dark screen room. Soon he will go along the corridor where he had searched for her and found her, bathing beside a candle among all those puppets . . . years ago. He cannot touch his own face because of the pain. He has no idea what he has broken.

After twenty minutes he gets up, puts on his clothes, and begins to attach the blasting caps onto the dynamite. He walks into the humidity of the pumping station. As he settles and beds the explosives he can see what will occur. A column of water will shoot up seventy feet into the air and break through the glass windows of the roof. The floor buckles, other pumps overload and burn out in seconds. When the settling basins explode, the military tents on the lawn above them will collapse downwards into twenty-four feet of pure water. He picks up the wheel of wire and lines the electrical fuses through the Venturi tunnels.

> "On the golf course I'm under par
> Metro-Goldwyn has asked me to star . . ."

The machine roar drowns him out as he half mutters half sings, unaware that the song from the boat has attached itself to him like a burr. He wades across the raw water of the filter pools with the wire wheel in his outstretched hand, selecting the key columns on which to lay the dynamite. The water from here will burst through the wired glass into the corridors of rosy marble.

> "I've got a house – a showplace
> Still I can't get no place – with you . . ."

He lays a charge with its electric detonator over the plaque that says Dominion Centrifugal Pump. The last ones he nestles under the ferric chloride tanks, and beside the rose marble tower clock with its code lights. He runs the wires into the blasting-box.

Barefoot, he walks up the staircase trailing the live wires behind him, around the mezzanine gallery and into Harris' office.

Harris sitting at his desk, the gooseneck lamp on, happens to be watching the door when it opens. Even if he had known the man before he would not recognize him now. Black thin cotton trousers and shirt, grease-black face – blood in the scrapes and scratches. The man's knuckles bleeding, one arm hanging loose at his side. He notices the shirt ripped open at the back when the intruder turns to close the door.

He walks towards Harris, the blasting-box carried like a chicken under his right arm.

– Do you know me?

– I worked for you, Mr. Harris. I helped build the tunnel I just swam through.

– Who are you? How dare you try to come in here!

– I'm not trying this, I've done it. Everything is wired. I just press the plunger on this blasting-box.

– What do you want? Who are you?

– I'm Patrick Lewis.

There was silence. Patrick leaned forward and rubbed his cut fingers over the smoothness of Harris' desk.

– Feldspar, he murmured.

Harris watched the eyes darting in the man's dark face. He walked over to the sideboard and returned with a decanter of brandy and glasses. He was thinking. Then he began to speak. He talked about how he hated the officials of the city but how he loved City Hall.

– I was practically *born* in City Hall. My mother was a caretaker. I worked up.

– You forgot us.

– I hired you.

– Your goddamn herringbone tiles in the toilets cost more than half our salaries put together.

– Yes, that's true.

– Aren't you ashamed of that?

– You watch, in fifty years they're going to come here and gape at the herringbone and the copper roofs. We need excess, something to live up to. I fought tooth and nail for that herringbone.

– *You* fought. *You* fought. Think about those who built the intake tunnels. Do you know how many of us died in there?

– There was no record kept.

– Turn off the light.

– What?

– Turn your light off.

Harris pulled the beaded cord on the gooseneck lamp. So the room was dark.

Patrick moved in shadow now, the blasting-box still under his right arm. He needed to stretch, to walk. He had been drowning in Harris' eyes and sleepy hand-movements, felt hypnotized by that calm voice, the solitary focus of the lamp. Without light he felt more awake, discerning shapes, the smell of a bed somewhere in the room. Harris spoke out of the darkness.

– You don't understand power. You don't like power, you don't respect it, you don't want it to exist but you move around it all the time. You're like a messenger. Think about it, Patrick. . . . No answer. I'll keep talking. But turn the light on before you decide to plunge that thing. Allow me that.

– I will. Just keep talking, Harris.

– What you are looking for is a villain.

Harris knew he had to survive until early morning. Then a column of sunlight would fall directly onto his large desk, the pad of grid paper, his fountain pen. His gun was by the bed. He had to survive till the first hint of morning colour came through the oculus above him, eight feet in diameter, made up of eight half-moons of glass. He leaned forward.

    – One night, I had a dream. I got off the bus at College – it was when we were moving College Street so it would hook up to Carlton – and I came to this area I had never been to. I saw fountains where there used to be an intersection. What was strange was that I knew my way around. I knew that soon I should turn and see a garden and more fountains. When I woke from the dream the sense of familiarity kept tugging me all day. In my dream the next night I was walking in a mysterious park off Spadina Avenue. The following day I was lunching with the architect John Lyle. I told him of these landscapes and he began to laugh. "These are real," he said. "Where?" I asked. "In Toronto." It turned out I was dreaming about projects for the city that had been rejected over the years. Wonderful things that were said to be too vulgar or expensive, too this, too that. And I was walking through these places, beside the traffic circle at Yonge and Bloor, down the proposed Federal Avenue to Union Station. Lyle was right. These *were* all real places. They could have existed. I mean the Bloor Street Viaduct and this building here are just a hint of what could have been done here.

You must realize you are like these places, Patrick.
You're as much of the fabric as the aldermen and the
millionaires. But you're among the dwarfs of enterprise
who never get accepted or acknowledged. Mongrel
company. You're a lost heir. So you stay in the woods.
You reject power. And this is how the bland fools – the
politicians and press and mayors and their advisers –
become the spokesmen for the age. You must realize the
trick is to be as serious when you are old as when you are
young.

> – Did you know a woman named Alice Gull?
> – No . . . should I?
> – Yes.
> – Is she dead?
> – Why do you say that?
> – You said *did*.
> – Yes.

Patrick turned the light on and saw Harris' eyes looking directly
into his.

> – Have you decided?
> – Not yet.

He switched off the light. Again they disappeared from each
other.

> – Alice Gull, Harris said very slowly, was killed by an
> anarchist.
> – No.
> – She was the actress. Is that correct?

In the darkness Patrick heard Harris sip his brandy and return the glass to the table. Patrick sat on the floor, his one good arm resting on the blasting-box.

– I think I saw her once, Harris said.
– She used to perform here. There used to be meetings in your unfinished waterworks. That's where I met her, after many years.
– What meetings? What do you mean?
– Then I lost her. . . . Someone gave her the wrong bag. A simple mistake. Picked up the wrong bag. So she was carrying dynamite with a timing device, a clock bomb. She was walking with it through the crowds along the Danforth, near Broadview, walking towards the centre of the city. Who knows what she thought she was carrying. They knew she was in danger as soon as it was discovered.

Patrick was almost inaudible, whispering. If he were writing this down, Harris thought, his handwriting would be getting smaller and smaller.

– I don't want to talk of this anymore.
– Then it will always be a nightmare.
– It *will* always be a nightmare, Harris. She had a line, an old saying. "In a rich man's house there is nowhere to spit except in his face."
– Diogenes.
– I don't know.

A silence.

– Patrick, talk to me.
– They found me at the tannery, screaming to me about what had happened. And I ran. I ran north along

239

the edge of the valley, no streetcars, all the demonstrations had caused chaos that day. I passed the Geranium Bakery and grabbed her friend Temelcoff to help find her. And the two of us ran all the way up to the Danforth where the crowd was, where she was supposed to be. By the time I got there, I had nothing in me to shout. *Alice!* I couldn't even whisper it. We kept leaping up to look for her over the heads of the crowd. She was carrying the clock bomb, not even knowing what it was, and soon everything she held would rocket out into her. Temelcoff and I jumped up and down, the mob around us, now and then seeing each other's frantic faces. . . . Then I heard the explosion. Not far away, near enough to have found her and picked up that bag and flung it anywhere else on the street. . . .

Then nobody moved, Patrick remembered, the whole crowd locked in stillness. There was already a distance between Alice bent over, holding her ribs, and the jolted people twenty feet away. As he came towards her she recognized him, her eyes indelible, the wound at her side.

He cradled her gently, he could hardly touch her without causing pain. Most of all he was holding her eyes with his, terrified they would close, would shut him out. One eye was flickering up and down, then the other, as if stuttering. Then the bag ten feet away exploded again.

Harmless. And when he looked back her eyes were closed. Her dead hand gripping the side of his jacket.

He got up and ran, her blood on him, along the horrified corridor in the crowd. The groan subconscious, slubbering out of his mouth. He banged into something very tough which brought his eyes back into focus.

He looked into the face of Temelcoff, who held him and wouldn't let go. Not to capture him but to calm him. Patrick struggling from side to side. The former bridge-builder's face held together only by the formality of two clear tears. Two little silver coaches.

Then Nicholas Temelcoff let him go and walked over to the body of Alice.

– Patrick . . .

There was a permanent darkness to the room. A permanent silence. Harris was still, quiet, unable to see. All he knew now was where the voice had been.

On the ceiling high above him was the window with eight half-moons. If he looked up in a while there would be a suggestion of blue. My god, he swam here, Harris suddenly realized. That's how he got in, through the tunnel. What vision, what dream was that? He pressed his repeater watch and it struck five. The sound fell clearly into the room.

The knowledge it would be daybreak soon kept Harris awake. He remained where he was during the next hour and by then the first light was in the room. It nestled in the corners of the ceiling, suggested cupboards, the damn herringbone that seemed to irritate everyone, and then it clarified the alcove where his bed was, where Patrick lay strangely – the lower half of his body crouched, knees drawn up, and the top half sprawled out, head back. There was blood across his neck and shirt. He had cut his throat in the darkness. My god. Harris got up. Then sat down again. No, he was asleep. He was asleep! The cuts old. From the journey here. Harris realized that he was relieved. The blasting-box was on the floor. Earlier Harris had understood why the man had chosen him, knew he was one of the few in power who had something tangible around him. But those with real power had nothing to show for themselves. They had paper. They didn't carry a cent. Harris was an amateur in their midst. He had to sell himself every time.

He stood over Patrick. "He lay down to sleep, until he was woken from out of a dream. He saw the lions around him glorying in life; then he took his axe in his hand, he drew his sword from his belt, and he fell upon them like an arrow from the string."

There was a knock on the door. Six o'clock. He said nothing. A knock again. Harris was concerned that Patrick would wake suddenly. "Come in," he whispered. An officer efficiently stepped in and saluted. Harris put his finger to his lips before the man could bark out information. He pointed to the man on the bed.

– Take that blasting-box and defuse it. Let him sleep
on. Don't talk. Just take it away. Bring a nurse with
some medical supplies here, he's hurt himself.

– Patrick?

He woke slowly, Hana's hand on his shoulder.

– Patrick? We have to go to Marmora.
– Five more minutes, ten more minutes.
– No, we *have* to go. I made a thermos of coffee
for us.
– Thank you.

He felt his clothes wet with the sweat of sleep.

– I'm awake. Marmora. Okay.

On the balcony in the night air, he peered down into the
landlord's long green garden. The last of the previous day's
heat was still in the atmosphere. Hana locked up and they went
down the two flights of metal stairway and then walked along
Albany Street towards the car. The houses at this hour beautiful and large, stray lights on within them, and he could see the
faint interiors, their privacy and character revealed, each room
a subplot. His good arm was around Hana's shoulder while she
hugged the thermos to her.

– Tell me about her.

243

– She was your mother's best friend. I'll tell you the
whole story.

The second-floor balconies curved out to the street. Odours
from each hedge. Mr. Rivera hosing his garden at three A.M.
having just returned from a night shift, private as they passed
him. A dog's chain hung off a step railing. They were off to
guide Clara back to this street. He found it most beautiful, felt
most comfortable at this hour when they often saw raccoons
pausing on steps, seemingly tamed, as if owning the territory of
the porch.

They stopped by the Ford and unlocked the passenger door.
He was about to climb over into the driver's seat.

> – Do you want to drive? he asked.
> – Me? I don't know the gears.
> – Go ahead. I'll talk the gears to you till we are out of
> town.
> – I'll try it for a bit.

Hana sat upright, adapting the rear-view mirror to her
height. He climbed in, pretending to luxuriate in the passenger
seat, making animal-like noises of satisfaction.

> – Lights, he said.